The Lakes
In My Head

The Lakes
In My Head

Paddling An Unexplored Wilderness

Lesli Chinnock Anderson

To order additional copies of this book, contact:
Xlibris
1-888-795-4274
www.Xlibris.com
Orders@Xlibris.com
757738

Table of Contents

PREFACE

I BRIEFLY TOUCH ON motherhood, parenting parents, depression, death, and hydrocephalus in this book. Please consult the resources I've listed at the end of the book for more information about these subjects. The Table of Contents is also set up so that it is easier to look up an event by chapter, in case the reader has a particular interest in one subject or another.

I have tried to keep the information here as factual as possible. Yet, one thing I've learned as I share my story with others is that people crave more than facts. We want to be reassured that we aren't alone in our experiences. We seek companionship on our journey. We seek hope.

With that in mind, I've included some of my perceptions along the way, and questions I've had on the trip. Keep asking questions. Don't give up. I hope sharing my experiences will help you to have less fear and more hope on your

unique pilgrimage.

Written with love for my husband Ken, daughter Kaitlyn, my mom

Marci, my brother Scott and sister-in-law Suzanne, and all my

cousins. And for all my paddling partners, wherever you are.

--LCA

PROLOGUE

Planning The Trip

NOT ALL OF life's twists and turns can be planned in advance.

Most of my wilderness adventures have been in the Boundary Waters Canoe Area of northeastern Minnesota. Before any paddling trip in the BWCA it is important to plan and map it out. Made up of living things, wilderness is fluid and constantly changing. If you are going to travel through wilderness, you must have the proper equipment for the unpredictable events you undoubtedly will encounter. You will need to secure a permit from the Department of Natural Resources. You will need shelter, enough food for the entire trip, suitable clothing, canoe paddling equipment. I usually pack too much clothing. I have a weakness for buying rain gear and polar fleece jackets similar to how some women have a weakness for shoes. When he goes camping my husband, Ken, has a weakness for technical gadgets, only packing clean clothing as an after-thought. Okay, that was unfair; I don't want you to get a bad impression of my husband. He would remember to pack clothing. He might not pack an extra shirt in case the one he's wearing gets splashed on or mauled by a black bear. (Just kidding. That's never happened to us.) Ken and I would also recommend that it is absolutely mandatory to leave a detailed plan of your trip with someone who can follow up should you unexpectedly encounter a situation you can't handle. Someone needs to know where to search for you if you become lost.

I have for many years wanted to write a book, to be an author, though I never thought I'd be writing about myself, which is what I'm about to do. This is an awkward task for me, because I have a disability that makes story-telling difficult. I keep forgetting where I am in the story.

I was sure, having an undergraduate Bachelor's degree in Biology with a minor in Chemistry, that my future writing would be about all things scientific: animals, plants, geography, ecology, caring for the environment, global warming, ornithology, canoe trips into vast uncharted wilderness, and topics like that.

Then, as my life continued on, I dabbled in inspirational writing. God has always been important in my life, even as a child. I tried combining writing about things biological and inspirational at the same time. Once, my work was published in a tiny, but well-distributed, devotional magazine. I guess the editors thought having an inspirational article about prayer and dolphins was different enough that people would read it and remember to pray. That's good. That's why I wrote it.

Though I spent almost twenty years working in several medical fields, any scientific facts I may have written about were already known and published, and I wasn't in research, though it interested me. Plus, scientific fields are surprisingly competitive and in order to have published work one has to make a breakthrough discovery.

Yet, I never gave up wanting to write, so from early on I have written regularly in a daily journal. Writing has always been therapeutic for me, a way to get my emotions and thoughts out of my head to make room for more emotions and thoughts. I am not an extrovert, so they pile up in my brain and heart, just waiting to be released. We all need to express ourselves and develop relationships with others. Sometimes those others are human, sometimes they are animals who travel the universe with us on this wonderful, green, oxygen-filled planet called Earth.

Now, however, I have a unique reason to write. I've paddled a unique route. Someone wiser than I mapped it out, and provided me with the resources I would need on the trip. This paddling route was the most arduous, challenging trip I've ever taken and I barely left my house to complete it.

CHAPTER ONE

The Drive North

THERE ARE MANY ways to get into the Boundary Waters Canoe Area. Getting there all depends on which direction you're coming from–Canada, the Dakotas, Wisconsin, or Iowa. I have lived in Minneapolis, Minnesota almost all of my life, so my trips usually began in the Twin Cities. To get to the BWCA, I usually drove north on Interstate 35W from the Twin Cities, through Duluth, along the North Shore of Lake Superior on Highway 61, to Grand Marais and Highway 12, otherwise known as The Gunflint Trail. Turning left onto it and proceeding in a westerly direction will take you into the BWCA.

There was one turn-off that did not appear on my map: when I was forty-five years old, I slipped and fell on a wet concrete floor while working in a veterinary hospital.

People all over the world, are interested in animals and love to keep them as pets. Veterinarians are people who love animals enough that they are willing to devote their lives to learning everything about them, and to pass on that knowledge to others who love animals and need advice on their care. I was concurrently working full-time and attending night school at a local technical college to earn a degree in Veterinary Technology. Veterinary technicians are amazing people. They are the equivalent of secretary, receptionist, care nurse, surgical nurse, emergency nurse, dental hygienist, laboratory technologist, dog-walker, janitor, animal wrangler, teacher, and funeral home employee all rolled into one, and all for a long list of animal species that are surprisingly different from one another. The same drug given to a dog requires a different dosage when given to a cat, not only because of their size difference, but because of their physiological differences. Cats metabolize drugs differently from dogs...and horses, and cattle, and birds, and turtles. Veterinary staff has to know that and care for each animal appropriately. That's a lot of knowledge to be responsible for.

So, while doing my job assisting the Veterinarians in the clinic where I worked, I walked too quickly to catch up to someone to whom I needed to speak, slipped on the freshly mopped clinic floor, and landed flat on my face. It was a concrete floor. This fall completely changed my life. My nose took most of the impact (thank you, Nose!) and it, of course, broke. While I was lying on my stomach, stunned and embarrassed, I began to laugh. I'm not sure why, except it was probably a reaction to the shock of finding myself on the clinic floor surrounded by about six staff members, all very worried about my condition. Lest you wonder, none of them were human medical doctors, so they really didn't know how to help me; they offered to take me to a human emergency department immediately.

I wanted my husband, Ken, nearby, so after he was called, I was driven to the (human) emergency department at the nearest hospital. X-rays showed I indeed did have a broken nose, and thankfully there was no sign of a concussion. They referred me to an ear-nose-and-throat physician for follow-up treatment.

My nose healed just fine, but inside my brain, something had changed. No one knew it at that time. I began to have more and more severe headaches, some lasting a few days. Over-the-counter pain medication did not help. My family doctor and I treated the pain with various medications for migraines. I had experienced headaches all my life, but these were much worse headaches than the ones I'd had growing up. Finally, in desperation I requested that a computed tomography, or CT scan be done of my sinuses to look for possible sinus infection or–Heaven forbid–a tumor.

Once a CT or CAT scan (boy, do I know some good jokes about Cat Scans!) is performed, a radiologist has to read the scan and interpret it. That is not as easy as one might think. CT uses x-rays to take pictures of your bones and the radiologist thereby interprets also what is in the spaces between the bones. Radiology may be a science, but it is truly also an art to read radiographs and it takes time to read them correctly. I had to wait a few days for the results of my scan.

Having some medical background and having taken radiographs of animals up until this time, my inquisitive mind tried to guess what the radiologist might find. This is never a good idea. It's far more peaceful to get on with your life and not try to diagnose yourself, yet all of us working in medicine have a tendency to do just that. I think it's the thrill of finding your guess was correct combined with the terror of knowing the worst thing it could turn out to be. Kind of like reading a mystery novel or riding a roller coaster in an amusement park. Days of waiting for test results are never any fun anyway, but some of us make it harder by giving in to our inquiring minds.

The call I received was not the one I was expecting. "You have a really nasty sinus infection" or "Your sinuses look normal" would have been nice to hear, though the headaches were so bad I was willing to hear, "You have cancer" just to get this over with and begin treatment. My family doctor said quietly over the phone, "You have no infection, Lesli. Your sinuses are clear." Then she paused before saying, "The radiologist found something he would like to get a better look at. Could you go in for a MRI scan?"

I calmly said, "Okay," but I knew deep down that radiologists don't view exposure to x-rays lightly. Physicians try to do as few x-rays as possible for that reason. And a MRI scan was a bigger procedure.

Magnetic resonance imagery uses giant magnets to take a series of pictures that the radiologist can put together to make a model of the body part in question. There was either something wrong or I had unusual sinuses. I went in for the MRI, then waited for the results. What could be so important that a radiologist would request a MRI? The hamster wheels in my inquisitive mind began to busily turn. I focused on my job and prayed nervously.

A few evenings later, while cleaning up at work after a long day, I received a phone call from my family physician. She apologized for calling me at work, saying, "You have hydrocephalus, Lesli, and the only treatment I know of is surgical placement of a shunt. I will refer you to a neurosurgeon so you can discuss it with him; he will know much more than I do."

Wow. What do you say to someone who's just told you you will likely need brain surgery? Thank you? Okay, no problem? Most people start with, "What is hydrocephalus?" but I already knew the answer to that.

I had heard of babies with "water on the brain", but not adults. How could this happen to me at 45 years old? This wasn't part of my trip plan; it wasn't even covered under contingencies. I had packed food, a tent, plenty of clothing and canoe paddles. How had I missed this?

CHAPTER TWO

Putting In At The Water's Edge

I BELIEVE A GEOGRAPHY lesson would be appropriate here. Stick with me and you'll see how this fits into my story. Minnesota is known as the Land of 10,000 Lakes and is the birthplace of the mighty Mississisippi River. I was born and raised in Minneapolis, one of the Twin Cities of Minneapolis and St. Paul. The Twin Cities metropolitan area is roughly in east-central Minnesota; Warroad, Minnesota, is almost as far north as you can go in the United States, except for Maine and Alaska. Minnesota is that place the meteorologists often say is the coldest location in the lower forty-eight states.

We love our more than 10,000 lakes and rivers here in Minnesota. We enjoy swimming, boating, fishing and scuba diving in the summer and snowmobiling, ice fishing, cross country skiing, downhill skiing, and snowboarding in the winter, in or on the lakes and rivers. Some (fool?) hardy residents even take the plunge by jumping into water surrounded by ice after warming up in a sauna. It started as a Scandinavian thing and many Minnesotans are of Scandinavian ancestry.

Living in Minneapolis, the City of Lakes, I reside near Lake Minnetonka, Lake Pamela, Lake Nokomis, Lake Hiawatha and the creek that connects all of them, Minnehaha Creek. Minnehaha means "curling waters" in the Native American Dahcota language, though it is frequently mistranslated as "laughing waters". The water from Minnehaha Creek becomes Minnehaha Falls, then empties into the Mississippi River which meets up with the Minnesota River and becomes the back bone of our country. The headwaters of the Mississippi, Lake Itasca in northern Minnesota southwest of the Boundary Waters Canoe Area in Itasca State Park, are not dramatic to behold. They trickle placidly and grow in strength as they flow south toward the Twin Cities. The mouth of the mighty Mississippi is way down South in New Orleans, Louisiana. That's a lot of water making a very long trip to the Gulf of Mexico. It mixes with saltwater from the ocean, forming a unique and special habitat known as an estuary. Estuaries are fascinating. Freshwater and saltwater wildlife live together, taking advantage of the ocean tides to obtain the nutrients they need to survive.

Along the way, that water is vitally important to the whole planet. The

United States relies very heavily on the Mississippi River to transport food and supplies. The river feeds a thirsty country. It provides essential habitat for birds, fish, crustaceans, insects, restless families in canoes...you get the picture. The water in the river evaporates into our air, fueling weather patterns. Nothing is wasted. Our economy is heavily dependent on the Mississippi River, and natural disasters like flooding effect how we all spend our finances. The Mississippi is written about in recreational books and textbooks. History has been made around it.

Next, a biology lesson.

Carefully protected inside the human head, inside your brain there are four compartments called ventricles. Filled with cerebrospinal fluid, they are connected by several narrow passageways and special cells. Cerebrospinal fluid, or CSF, flows between the two lateral ventricles, down to the third ventricle, through the Aqueduct of Sylvius (also called the cerebral aqueduct), and down further into the fourth ventricle, then into the narrow space surrounding the brain and the spinal cord. The CSF that bathes our brains provides important nutrients to the neurons and spinal column. It helps clean out cellular waste, and protects us by filling the space between our brains and our skulls with an absorptive cushion of fluid. Without it we would experience major brain trauma each time we bumped our heads.

Our bony skulls act as armor. Newborn babies have a soft spot, the anterior fontanel, where the skull has not finished growing together. Their brains are protected in that spot by a membrane that covers the hole. Soon after birth, the hole disappears and in its place is a completed bony skull. As the baby grows and matures, the brain and skull grow and mature as well. Once the CSF has made the rounds, so to speak, through the whole system, it is expelled from the brain by special cells, and absorbed into our bodies. Nothing is ever wasted.

Hydrocephalus (hi' dro sef' uh luhs-- from two latin words meaning "water" and "head") occurs when something prevents the CSF from freely flowing in the "lakes and creeks and rivers" inside the head. Yes, that was the reason for the geography lesson, not to mention it was fun to tell it to you. I am proud to be a Minnesotan. Imagine what would happen if Minnehaha Creek or the Mississippi River was damned up by beavers. Where would the water go? It would overflow its banks and flood the surrounding land, maybe even spilling over the top of the dam. Though CSF may be impeded by an obstruction in an aqueduct, it continues to be produced at the rate of 0.35 milliliters per minute and flows through the system anyway. In babies, because their skulls are not yet knit together completely, the CSF pushes against the brain, causing the skull to expand to accommodate the fluid. The anterior fontanel may bulge or be abnormally convex. The pressure inside the brain increases abnormally. In teenagers and adults, whose skulls are complete, the extra pressure builds as the fluid has no where to go, so it presses against brain cells, causing pain and problems for normal cell function.

This may cause urinary incontinence, mobility abnormalities, cognitive and language learning disabilities, and severe headaches. These are not tension or sinus headaches, mind you, easily relieved with a convenient pill. These are excruciating headaches, like migraine headaches, and no over-the-counter medication will suffice.

Common causes of hydrocephalus include congenital lesions (e.g., spina bifida), traumatic lesions (concussions), and infections such as meningoencephalitis, as well as congenital aqueductal stenosis and a rare genetic disease. One form of hydrocephalus can be misdiagnosed as Alzheimer's Disease or Parkinson's Disease. Usually, neurosurgeons can tell you which type of hydrocephalus you have and how best to treat it.

So, back to my evening phone conversation at the vet clinic. Here I am standing with a phone in my hand, listening to a doctor whom I trust, thinking about all these tidbits of medical information and pondering, "Me? Really? Hydrocephalus? Now what do I do?" At least I knew what it was. Many people don't. Plus it's really hard to spell and pronounce. It's a good thing I enjoy learning languages, like medical Latin.

What next? With help from my family physician, I chose my neurosurgeon wisely–I looked on the internet, not the best source of accurate scientific information. But by God's grace the site I chose to search was a good one. Choosing a neurosurgeon is like choosing a mechanic for your car. Most people try to choose wisely, knowing they would like their investment to last as long as possible. Surgeons are detail oriented, precise, and not necessarily very chatty. They know their subjects inside and out, and they have fantastic memories for spacial organization in the body. They are also very coordinated with tools. I am not. I would not make a good surgeon. Nor a mechanic.

Neurosurgeons are the cream of the crop when it comes to surgeons. They rank right up there with cardiac surgeons; they have to. Our brains and our hearts are, physically, what give us life. The neurosurgeon I selected is nationally known and had even appeared on a popular magazine cover, but that wasn't why I chose him. I also didn't choose him for his service prices. One should never choose medical care based on price. He had many years of experience performing surgery on people with hydrocephalus, both children and adults. I scheduled an appointment with him, and given my situation the clinic got me an appointment right away. I was grateful for that. I really didn't want to endure anymore headaches.

The appointment was scary, no doubt about that. The surgeon wasn't scary; he had a confident yet gentle, and soft-spoken demeanor. He told me I was not alone. At first I thought that was an odd thing to say, but as I pondered it I realized I do feel alone. After all, I am the only one inside my head. He was willing to answer every one of my questions. I had a long list. He actually gently took my list from my hands and read each question quickly, saying "yes" or "no" in response, giving a short explanation if needed. He didn't ignore a single question. What I needed to know so badly, he couldn't tell me for sure.

I asked, "Do I have hydrocephalus because I fell and hit my head?" His answer was an immediate, "No." "So, I had to be born with it and no one knew it was there?" I asked. He nodded his head yes. He had seen a lot of cases of hydrocephalus, I reminded myself. He should know. He showed me the MRI images of my brain, and specifically, the colorful hour glass shaped Aqueduct of Sylvius connecting the lateral and third ventricles with the fourth ventricle. Do you recall my lesson on Minnehaha Creek and the four lakes it connects? Do you remember the beavers? Well, *my* Aqueduct of Sylvius was shaped like an hour glass. It wasn't supposed to be. There was a stenosis, or narrowing of the flow, right in the middle and the fluid had backed up on either side of the stenosis, creating an hour glass shape where there was supposed to be a straight, open canal. The surgeon said this particular condition, aqueductal stenosis, is almost always congenital. I was born with it. The beavers had been busy during my gestation in the womb.

I was in disbelief. How could I have had hydrocephalus for forty-five years without anyone knowing it?

The solution, I was told, was to surgically place a shunt in my brain to drain off the excess CSF. A ventriculoperitoneal shunt is a long silicone catheter placed with one end in one of the lateral ventricles, sliding the other end under my skin all the way down to my peritoneal cavity. The end in my brain (the anterior end) would have a one way valve on it that could be set to open when the pressure in the ventricles reached a predetermined setting. Then, fluid would travel down the catheter and be absorbed in my peritoneal cavity, the space in which the lower half of my internal organs lies. The valve setting would control how much CSF is allowed to travel down the catheter and when.

"So, we should schedule your surgery soon."

Brain surgery? But this was not on my agenda, my life's plan!

As a teenager I'd dreamed of observing animal behavior some place like Africa or Canada. I'm aware that most people don't put those countries in the same category. I didn't either. I started wanting to go to Africa to observe lions and cheetahs and chimpanzees. As I grew older and continued to have headaches from the humid Minnesota summer heat, I switched my dream to some place cooler, like Alaska or Canada to see polar bears and whales and Arctic wolves. Over and over again I had asked God in prayer to help me find the right career for myself. When I entered college at Bemidji State University, a degree for "animal behavior observer" had not been established. Now there are degrees available in animal psychology and animal behavioral sciences. I'd considered getting a PhD and going on to become a university professor, or becoming a park naturalist in a state or national park, a medical technician or a physical therapist. I had finally settled on earning a second degree in Veterinary Technology. It had taken about five years post-college and numerous tries applying to schools, taking entrance tests and additional classes to get to this point. I had waded through refusals and disappointing interviews, all while working full-time in medical laboratories and veterinary clinics.

I'd completed two internships at the Minnesota Zoo, one in education, the other working with the marine mammals (dolphins, in this case). I knew all the scientific names of the marine mammals most frequently found in zoos and aquariums; I wrote an unpublished paper on dolphin food choices that the staff decided to refer to in the future, and my educational dolphin toy was a hit. My husband helped me construct it: it was a pool float connected to a section of PVC pipe with a door on it that opened in response to a stimulus, in this case a dolphin's rostrum or mouth. The dolphins only had to use their sonar capability to "see" that we'd put fish inside the pipe, then figure out how to open the door. Cool, huh? My husband is really adept with tools and he'd worked with sonar.

Is it really possible, that all or some of those headaches I experienced as a child and adult may have been due to an unknown congenital condition? That over the years my brain had compensated for it unbeknownst to anyone else? That my nasty fall on wet concrete upset the delicate balance of my brain?

I had always been an A or B student, and never had any problems with learning. Is it possible that my mind had known of the defect in my brain, and compensated for it completely on its own?

Amazingly, just a few weeks earlier, feeling bored with my life and frustrated by my financial and medical problems, I'd said to a co-worker, "I wish I would get a really big surprise—a happy one, out of the blue—I love surprises..." What struck me at the time was that in those simple words I was really voicing one of my deepest desires. I was praying for reassurance that this life journey I was traveling on with all its pain and frustrations was really worth the effort.

Eventually, it dawned on me that this surgery was my answer to prayer and I was at peace with the idea of it. It also became evident that my choices were 1.) horrible headaches indefinitely or 2.) surgery with the hope that the pressure in my head would be relieved. I decided to take the second option and trust God, the Great Physician.

Life doesn't always happen as planned. This is why it's so important to leave a copy of your travel plans with someone before you depart on your journey!

CHAPTER THREE

Lake One: The Beauty of Paddling In Sync

ONCE A BWCA trip is planned, it is time to prepare the equipment. Check out the canoe and the tent for tears or leaks. Ensure there is enough food packed for the entire trip, but not so much that it can't be carried in a pack. Then there's the drive north and wondering if you remembered to pack everything. When you finally arrive at the starting point of your journey, unload the canoe and equipment from the car, and put in, you feel joy as you realize the journey that took so much work to prepare for has begun. Your paddles dip in sync as your craft glides gracefully through the clean, clear water.

Fortunately, up to this point, I had undergone quite a few surgeries in my life. I no longer owned a gallbladder, for one, so I was not too worried about the thought of undergoing surgery in general. I'd assisted in numerous animal surgeries and procedures requiring anesthesia. I was fairly familiar with anesthesia, how it worked and how I'd feel when waking up from it.

For someone without these experiences, I can't imagine how it must feel to be anticipating brain surgery. It must be terrifying, to say the least.

I was nervous, though; after all, poking and prodding in my brain would be a serious and potentially life-threatening event. Thankfully, I had a rich spiritual and prayer life, and I was surrounded by friends and family who supported me in prayer. I would be given a sedative, prepared for surgery in a surgery prep room, and I would wake up with a little pain and some holes in my head and abdomen. I am eternally grateful for all the hospital staff who assisted in the preparation and in the surgery itself; I knew from experience that there was a lot of detailed, precise thought and work that went into performing a surgery.

One evening, while lying in bed, my husband turned and looked me in the eye and said he was worried I would die in surgery. I looked him in the eye right back, smiled, and said, "I'm not. I'm not afraid of death. I know Heaven exists and I will be there with Jesus if I die. I also have been through enough surgeries to know what will be happening to me. I can't guarantee I will live, but I can guarantee I will be fine."

It is not the purpose of this book to describe the surgery in detail, but there is a list of helpful resources at the end, if someone was interested in knowing more. Many people have written very helpful volumes of information on surgery for hydrocephalus; these are far more qualified than I to lead a person through the surgical procedure.

Not including all the prep and post-operation care, the surgery took about an hour.

I woke up from anesthesia (yes, Ken! I woke up! Yay!) in the post-op room, with just a little pain in my head, a little less hair than the day before, and feeling quite groggy. The nurses were attentive, regularly asking me how much pain I had, trying to assist me in coming out of anesthesia, while still trying to keep me drugged enough to not feel much pain. Pain is interesting. It tells us when something needs to be paid attention to in our bodies, but too much of it will actually impede healing.

While in the neurology unit of the hospital, I repeatedly dozed off from the pain medication. During one of these naps, I had an amazing dream. I dreamed that I was walking, stumbling around as if drunk, in a nice residential neighborhood with parks and trees. At each corner, when I needed to cross the street, one of my many friends from the past was waiting there to give me assistance. My friends were appearing out of nowhere to help me, smiling and chuckling as they did.

It made me feel surrounded by love.

It's the kind of love you feel when you and your partner are paddling on a smooth, glassy lake, your paddles dipping into the placid water at exactly the same moments, albeit on opposite sides of the canoe. It's a dance on water, performed with one partner in the bow, one in the stern, switching sides in a rhythm that can only be felt by those who have been there.

CHAPTER FOUR

The First Portage: A Heavy Weight

*P*ORTAGE: 2. A) a carrying of boats and supplies overland from one lake or river to another, as during a canoe trip b) any route over which this is done.

Portaging a canoe and packs takes practice and muscle, but once you get the hang of it, it's rewarding to hoist the canoe over your head. It can take many canoe trips to "get the hang of it", but you will undoubtedly get better and better as you develop your back, arm and shoulder muscles. Practice, practice, practice.

Surgery was on a cold Monday in March of 2007, and by Friday I felt well enough to go home from the hospital. Many people are able to go home much sooner, but I have always taken longer to recover from anesthesia.

Following brain surgery, I had sutures and lumps on my scalp where the shunt was visible under the skin, and part of my head was shaved. No more severe headaches. The relief was monumental. I did experience slight skull pain, neck pain, dizziness and a little nausea. A strange tingling in my tongue reminded me I'd just had brain surgery. I was sleepy from the pain meds and from head trauma, and spent most of my time simply lying down or sitting up in bed. I reluctantly got out of bed and walked around the neurology unit, which was quite pleasant. It had been decorated with comfortable family-sized visiting areas and a beautiful, artistic fountain.

For weeks following the surgery, a slight headache or a "full" feeling in my head were present off and on. My eyes were sensitive to light and my tongue continued to tingle. I walked around the neighborhood for exercise and to help heal my coordination. I was not allowed to lift anything, because that physical action increases pressure to the brain. Every activity that we take for granted—eating, sleeping, walking, rising from a seated position—required a little more concentration than usual. We take so much for granted. My brain allows me to be. To talk, to walk, to listen, to laugh, to think, to feel, to touch, the list is endless. My brain contains who I am. What an incredible thought. We talk about feeling with our hearts, but truly, physiologically, what we feel starts with our brains. Our bodies are absolutely awesome.

About a week after surgery I wrote in my journal:

"Today I'm going to walk to the grocery store for toilet paper, and perhaps walk to the aquarium store with my daughter, Kaitlyn to pick out new fish (now that King Arthur has died and no longer murders other fish in Camelot)."

It's a long story. My career NOT as an aquarist was decided early on when we began keeping fish. We seem to do much better with mammals. At this time we had a small aquarium, three cats and three rescued birds, a yellow and grey cockatiel named Alec, and two parakeets. Oh, and all my house plants. No, they didn't have names, but they were important to me. Caring for the whole crew and my human family gave me a meaningful schedule to follow every day. They all needed to be fed and watered daily.

It became evident that *I* needed to drink more water, a lot more water, like liters more water. No one seemed to know why, so I just did it because it felt good. Time alternately felt too slow, then too fast. Sometimes I wondered if I'd be ready to go back to work in April. Sometimes I wondered why I couldn't just go back to work now. How was I going to keep up with my thirst while at work?

At the four-week surgery follow-up appointment with Stephanie, my nurse practitioner at the neurosurgeon's office, I had a migraine headache. She ordered a CT Scan, which we then discussed. I ended the appointment by throwing up in her office. The CT confirmed that there was still inflammation from surgery around my shunt valve and along the edge of the brain on my surgery side. The ventricles appeared to be draining too quickly, so she placed a magnetic device next to my shunt, changing the pressure setting on my valve to a higher setting, allowing the ventricles to retain more CSF. This was a normal adjustment to have to make following surgery, since it can take time to discern just how filled with fluid is normal for each person receiving a shunt. This seemed to do the trick, and I had only a slight headache by the next day. The nausea was gone. It was such a relief!

On a Sunday early in May, I wrote in my journal:

"On Wednesday I saw the nurse practitioner at my neurosurgeon's office and we did a CT scan of my brain. I am doing well! And all of my restrictions are lifted. No signs of inflammation on the scan. Ventricles look good, not too small, not too large. I am free to go back to work. I am on the schedule starting tomorrow.

"A team from the vet clinic at which I worked walked the five-mile Humane Society Walk for Animals. Our Administrative Veterinarian matches all donations, so the total contribution was $12,000.00. I contributed a small amount and walked the entire walk. It was a very humid day, with thunderstorms hitting us by 1:00 pm. I did well, until the rain came and I realized how tired I was.

"I took over-the-counter sinus medication before the walk and again at 2:00 pm. I'm not sure it helped, although I was outside for about four hours. By the time I got home I was headachey and slightly nauseated. I believe the nausea was from not enough food in my stomach and swallowing the medication. I threw up all afternoon and part of the night. Much of it was 'dry heaves'. The headache stayed until early morning. All of this happened yesterday, so today I am exhausted. I think the five miles was about double the distance I have been walking since surgery, so I probably did a little too much yesterday, but I felt like I had to do it.

"Wearing a hat in the wind seems to be important, too. The wind really bothered my head, and it was extremely windy.

"I am so nervous about work tomorrow. Will I make it through a day? I'm afraid I'll get tired. I am already experiencing 'homesickness' as I think about the hours I won't be with Kaitlyn, or free to do something with Ken."

The world didn't stop for me while I had surgery and recovered. Imagine that! During this time, my mother, Marci, and mother-in-law, Justine, were having medical issues, as well, and they required Ken and I to be present with them at least part of the time. In and out of hospitals, we tried to remain sane. In the midst of this, one of our cats, Heidi, began vomiting. She had to be taken to the vet clinic for an anesthetized dental cleaning, during which she lost most of her teeth due to a feline syndrome where a cat will reabsorb its teeth. Our daughter, Kaitlyn, thirteen years old and thinking she was eighteen, was in the midst of her own challenges when many of her teachers decided to leave her school right in the middle of her middle school years.

It was a time of challenge and transition for the whole family. Oh, and I began the extended process of going through menopause. And discovered

I was lactose intolerant. Do you know how hard it is to live without dairy products when milk is one's favorite drink?

By mid-May, Heidi was healing and eating well. I was having occasional headaches. My job was going well and I didn't have to be preoccupied with wondering when I was going to get the next headache. My co-workers seemed glad to have me back, asking me if I felt better than before the surgery. My answer was yes. I do! It amazed me that there are people in the universe who say they have never had a headache. I can't imagine what that would be like. What freedom that would be!

It amazed me that I had had only two or three severe headaches during the last three months. No migraines, no migraine medication. Still, by the 29th of May, my cranial (head) incision had not completely healed. It oozed pus. (eww. Too much information, right?)

On May 31st, my neurosurgeon examined my cranial incision, which was still oozing and scabbing. I was told this could be from an infection or inflammation under the skin, but not in the shunt. The doctor wanted to "revise the incision", meaning to open up the wound and examine the shunt and tissues again. This type of infection could lead to shunt infection, which would lead to meningitis and hospitalization and/or removal of the shunt.

Meanwhile, at work it was getting harder and harder to request time off for doctor appointments and sick time. I was not alone; others with on-going medical concerns were having the same experience. Our manager and I had some heated discussions.

In my journal I wrote:

"All aspects of the surgical incision revision went well. I stayed overnight Tuesday and came home from the hospital Wednesday afternoon. I am disliking the post-anesthesia recovery process more and more; medicine does a wonderful job of giving me effective drugs to guard against nausea, vomiting and pain, but nothing makes healing go any faster except rest and prayer. And nothing makes my manager more understanding about my absences from work.

"I took a bath for the first time since Monday; it feels so good to be warm and clean. I've washed my hair twice, trying to keep my stitches dry.

"Linda called and we talked about an hour this morning. It's good to keep in touch with friends. Karyl called yesterday.

"I feel so many emotions. *Thankfulness* and *love* toward God my Father and my friends and family. *Weariness* from surgeries. *Sadness* that my family has to adjust their lives for me. *Worry* about the future—work, school, Kaitlyn's school situation. *Loneliness*—going into pre-op is a very lonely feeling. Recovering feels lonely, too, at times. *Empathy* for one of our other cats, Gretchen, who had an anesthetized dental cleaning and tooth extractions yesterday. Recovering from anesthesia just so stinks! *Anger* that I had to go through another surgery Tuesday. Anger that employers can't be more understanding. Anger that teacher shuffling is already happening at Kaitlyn's school. *Weariness of my soul.* I feel like the anger is weighing me down."

Carrying extra, unnecessary weight when you are portaging makes the walk more difficult. You tire more easily. In the BWCA, you can't just drop extra weight, leaving it on the ground to pick up later. This is why careful planning is essential, but if needed you can always break your gear down into smaller groupings and make several trips to get all the way through that portage.

CHAPTER FIVE

Lake Two: Developing Muscle

WE NAME LAKES after a variety of things. Wildlife we see there (Seagull Lake, Gull Lake, Kingfisher Lake, Moose Lake, Sora Lake, Auk Lake, and Owl Lake). Native descriptions of the lake (Cherokee, Saganaga, Ogishkemuncie, Gabimichigami, Makwa, and Kekekabic). Someone we know, or even ourselves (Jerry, Mora, Thelma, Annie, Jenny, Eddy, Fraser, Thomas). Something we ate (Noodle Lake). How we felt upon arrival (Snub, Sniff, Crooked and Tickle). Geological features (Snowbank, Frost, Alpine, and Jasper). Our survival equipment (Gunflint, Knife, and Hatchet Lakes). It is a human trait to name our surroundings, and certainly a useful one. Communication is much easier when both parties know what they are talking about.

Each lake in the Boundary Waters has its own personality. Some have rocky shorelines, from previous glacial activity in Northern Minnesota and Canada. Some have swampy shorelines making it hard to find a good place to land your canoe. Some lakes have large submerged rocks out in mid-lake that are fun to stand on while someone takes your photo because it looks like you're walking on water. Some just have a peaceful feel that you can't really put your finger on. Some are shallow with lots of dangerous submerged rocks that could damage your canoe.

By mid-June, I couldn't believe I'd spent the entire Spring recovering and resting.

I had mixed feelings about being back at work. I was angry with the whole veterinary profession. The veterinary profession, like a lot of professions, exists between a rock and a hard place. Vet clinic employees love animals and enjoy caring for them, but care costs money. Supplies and testing equipment cost money. They don't want to see their animal friends go without medical care, so they lower the prices they charge just enough to make it easier for pet owners. The veterinarians want to be able to pay their employees enough to make a living and give them benefits like health care and sick time. But it is a professional field with employees that require education and experience, and of course that costs money, too. Clinic managers expect that when they hire someone, their sick time will be minimal, since it requires consistent and faithful employees to run a high-quality practice.

I understood those issues, but I was having extreme medical experiences beyond my control. I didn't want to request leave and sick time; but I had to. Wouldn't anyone sympathize with me? Work continued to be a challenge. I felt like I was on secret probation.

In my prayers, I cried out to God,"God, You seem a million miles away. I haven't been able to feel Your presence since I became angry. I couldn't even praise You with my heart today in worship, and that doesn't happen often. Where are You?"

My revised cranial incision healed nicely. I wore a baseball-style cap at work to keep me from touching my head with contaminated hands. I noticed several subtle changes since I'd had the shunt placed. No more migraines or migraine medications. No more preoccupation with planning for the next headache. I felt freedom. My memory was better: by the end of the day, I could clearly remember where I'd parked my car that morning. I could multi-task more easily.

Growing up, I remember not liking to drink water. Now, I had to have it. I couldn't live without drinking at least 40-48 ounces of fluids daily.

By the beginning of August, I'd begun night school again. It was taxing, but I was looking forward to the completion of my veterinary technician degree. It made my work so much more interesting to know more of what was going on around me. I was thankful God was helping to make my road less rocky. I opted to receive a series of two rabies vaccines as part of my vet tech training; the vaccinations made me very sleepy. Rabies virus elicits a strong immune response and many people feel tired and sick after receiving the vaccines.

In the back of my mind, (or more accurately, on the middle left side of my mind...) I was always wondering if my shunt was healthy.

In the Veterinary profession, we are exposed to a lot of interesting parasites and bugs. We come in contact with urine and feces; are hissed at, licked, and scratched; and sometimes vomited upon–you name it. (I once mentioned that to someone who worked in pre-school child care and she turned to me and said, "Me, too!") I'd always looked at those dangers as just a part of working with animals. Still, one does what one can to avoid the dangers, if possible. In spite of taking precautions, I contracted ringworm from some cute kittens at tech school and was put on miconazole, an anti-fungal agent, as a precaution. About the same time, I was put on prednisolone (related to prednisone, a corticosteroid to reduce inflammation) for persistent jaw pain from having a breathing tube during my brain surgery. To my great relief, both healed up rather nicely.

On September 10th, I wrote:

"Well, I'm officially 46 years old now. I had a wonderful, quiet birthday. Our church's Praise Team sang 'Happy Birthday' to me twice, once at rehearsal and once during the Sunday worship service. Even Ken and Kaitlyn sang for me, and took me out to dinner at a restaurant. The three of us spent the whole day together, just doing normal family things: we bought wood chips for the backyard and spread them out together. We ate together. We slept in together. It was very nice. Kaitlyn even bought me a beautiful pin from the Science Museum of Minnesota in the likeness of a chickadee, all on her own—a complete surprise....Kaitlyn and I also walked up to the aquarium store and bought a new addition to our tank. Mind you, this is the tank she once said she wasn't interested in anymore. I wanted a big, brightly colored fish to add to the beauty of the tank. She wanted something more interesting. So, because she was showing so much renewed interest in the aquarium, we purchased a fiddler crab. We named her Tinkerbell, Tink for short. We also bought a water testing kit so we can test our own water instead of taking samples up to the aquarium store. Kaitlyn enjoyed helping with the first testing of the new tank. She is continuing to enjoy science. I wonder what she'll do in her adult life. Will she go to art school? Will she follow her mom and go into science? Will she work at a book store? She loves to read; she spends hours and hours reading book after book."

I'd been on several daily medications for many years. Given the recent changes in my brain, my family doctor decided to see, one trial at a time, which of my daily medications could be discontinued. We also treated my recurring sinus infections. We determined, over months of trial and error, that I still need my anxiety-depression medication and my SVT medication.

What? Oh! What is SVT? SVT—short for supraventricular tachycardia. Long before my brain became the center of attention, I was having episodes of supraventricular tachycardia. Okay, let's break this down linguistically: supra—a prefix that means above, over or on the top side.

ventricular—pertaining to a small cavity; one of the cavities of the brain filled with cerebrospinal fluid, or *either of two lower chambers of the heart that, when filled with blood, contract to propel it into the arteries. The right ventricle forces blood into the pulmonary artery and thence into the lungs; the left pumps blood into the aorta to the rest of the body.*

tachy—meaning rapid

cardia—meaning heart

I had been having episodes of rapid, strong heart beat which centered above one of my heart ventricles, ever since I was a kid. Especially on those hot, humid days when I also had headaches. It had been determined that these were not life-threatening, just annoying. My doctor and I wanted to see if relieving my brain of hydrocephalus would cause my SVT's to stop occurring. It didn't and they still do occur when I'm not on the medication.

I continued assisting at the vet clinic, working on my degree evenings and weekends. I made it through finals week at school. Another quarter of school out of the way!

Headaches were becoming more and more common for me, and in October, two of my co-workers contracted viral meningitis, a highly contagious infection of the tissues of the brain. I was afraid to go to work, afraid I might contract the virus, too.

One extra-curricular activity that was important to my health was singing at my church. Music is wonderfully healing, both to hear and to produce, and it requires the use of my whole brain. It is holistic healing. One evening each week, our Praise Team sang and put together music for our worship service. The Praise Team was singers and instrumental musicians, all having a passion for approaching God with music.

Near the end of October, while helping Kaitlyn install new bedroom furnishings that she had chosen herself on a shopping trip, I blew up at her. I'd told both Ken and Kaitlyn many times to pick up their belongings all over the house, but they didn't do it, or they would promise to do it at a future time or date. This was certainly just normal family life, but I was overwhelmed with stress and my patience was thin. Praise Team at church was becoming more stressful than I preferred, as well, and my parents and mother-in-law continued needing many hours of attention. They had spent many hours and much labor loving us, so I wanted to love them in return.

I wrote: "Is this what a nervous breakdown feels like? Overwhelming anger, needing to sleep for three-hour naps, being so upset one cries for hours?" I had a sound like a field of crickets in my head. I began to question what normal is, and one morning I couldn't remember taking my calcium pill while I was drinking the water to swallow it down. That can't possibly be normal, I thought. It was time to visit the doctor–again.

Both my neurologist and my family doctor agreed that my shunt and ventricles looked fine. My symptoms seemed to be medication-related. We did some tweaking of my medications (as my husband likes to say). I could rejoice and be thankful that my shunt was healthy and I was on fewer medications than I'd been on a year before.

Kaitlyn was turning a year older and had begun the process of choosing which high school she wanted to attend. She was attending a summer program for youth with higher learning expectations. She was singing in a youth choir and playing in a handbell choir at church. She was, and is, a person who takes initiative. For me at this time, that was a tremendous blessing. She knew how to care for herself.

Mine and my family's life was like a BWCA lake: a few submerged rocks to watch out for, and the mosquitoes and flies could be annoying, but it was worth the effort to experience the beauty and peace of wilderness.

CHAPTER SIX

The First Camp Site

I N ORDER TO maintain the wilderness aspect of the BWCA, the law requires campers to set up their equipment only in designated camp sites. The sites are not as luxurious as camp sites at a national or state park. They are rustic, usually consisting of a lightly cleared spot for a tent, and not much more. There may be an open-air pit toilet nearby, deep in the woods for privacy. In the wilderness, that's all anyone needs. Just the basics. Responsible campers leave it cleaner and better than when they arrived. Finding a good camp site near the end of a strenuous day of paddling or portaging is reason for celebration. It energizes and rejuvenates tired muscles and joints.

I had not written in my journal for about two months; I had neither the urge nor the time to write. I took vacation time from work. This was one of those use-it-or-lose-it vacations. So, I decided to use it for getting "caught up". I filled out insurance paperwork, began stripping wallpaper in the kitchen, got lots of sound sleep, ate well, took all my medications and vitamins, did yoga stretches regularly, helped my mom-in-law who lived alone in a house clean up her mail and paperwork mess, read a book, spent quite a lot of time with Praise Team and at church, and allowed my mind and heart to clear. Two of our cats, Heidi and Princess, went to the vet and received a clean bill of health, though Heidi would need another dental cleaning soon. In all, it was a vacation away from work, but not from life. Kaitlyn and I even spent some time together. She had begun scrapbooking!

My mom-in-law, Justine, whom I love dearly, had spent much of her life like others of her post-world-war generation, collecting stuff. She also had a habit that I could giggle about. She had forgotten about little stashes of mail "to look at later." Literally all over her house. Each time I visited her, I'd try to find all of the piles and we would go through them together. We discovered some important things in the process. We enjoyed each other's company, we were alike in interesting ways, she was becoming extremely forgetful, and she loved to give her money away to compassionate organizations. We had some good, heart-to-heart talks about how to prevent the clutter from piling up again, and being careful to whom and how often she should donate her money. We knew that if she continued to be so forgetful, we would need to focus on her need for assistance.

We continued to push her gently but firmly in the direction of reducing her material possessions. She was and is very traditional and sentimental, so the process of letting go was excruciating for her. Her whole upbringing was directed toward collecting things and preparing to hand them down to her beloved children (she has three, plus their significant others and some grandchildren). Emotionally, she wasn't yet ready to hand them down. We settled on putting post-it notes on the underside of objects to remind her to whom she wanted to give them...some day.

Meanwhile, Ken and I had settled on a pale shade of green for two of the kitchen walls and a slightly darker shade of green for the other two walls. My vision was for the room to feel like Spring. Greens, flowers, photos of water, an Easter cross, an aquarium with live fish and a fountain, Asian calligraphy-- similar to a Japanese garden, when one uses his or her imagination.

My coursework that week was light on assignments, which worked out well with my vacation time. By now, I was a little more than half way through school.

One of the activities I enjoyed during this time was pet sitting for others. It gave me hands-on experience with other's pets in preparation for my career. An entry from my journal dated March of 2008 says, "Emma is spending a few days with us. [Emma is an adorable Yorkshire Terrier who lives in our neighborhood. She was rescued from an abusive home by my compassionate and generous neighbor.] She brings with her enthusiasm, friendliness, and humility. She is also making me keep to a consistent schedule, which is hard to do with a sleep disorder--I frequently take naps. Today's great news is that my acquaintance from church, for whom we've been praying, received a hydrocephalus brain shunt! He and I have had many discussions about my shunt. His shunt is a blessing; he is doing well and he loves his shunt! How cool is that!"

Sleep disorder, you ask? "Good grief," you exclaim, "aren't we done with medical diagnoses?" Six years before this I had been diagnosed with sleep apnea. We'd tried using a Continuous Positive Air Pressure machine at that time, but I couldn't tolerate having a mask on my face connected to a hose while I slept. For some reason, unlike others who'd tried a CPAP machine, I was not immediately relieved and happy to be sleeping peacefully. I'd tried SCUBA diving back when I'd been interning at the Zoo with the dolphins and had a similar experience. I disliked having my face covered even if it was a way to breathe. Fortunately, the seizure medication I'd been on to help my headaches actually also helped me sleep more soundly, so I was choosing not to use my CPAP machine at this time.

Also at this time, I was finding it healing to share my hydrocephalus experience with others. It helped me put my whole life into perspective. It created lots of questions I wanted to answer, puzzles for me to put together. Mysteries to attempt to solve.

As a family, we needed to choose which high school Kaitlyn would go to for ninth grade. The Minneapolis public school system at this time had a choice process that also involved a lottery and specific criteria set up by the school board. We filled out the application, and Kaitlyn made her choice. When she and her friends received the school board's choice for them, it wasn't what they'd requested. She had been assigned to our neighborhood high school, but we as a family decided it would not be a good choice for her. She was coming from a school that had just made huge staff changes and was now assigned to a high school also in the midst of huge changes in teaching staff. Considering what she had to go through and all that was happening in our family, we wanted her to go to a school she felt really good about. She has always been an exceptionally perceptive individual, sensitive to the social environment in which she operates. So, we began the appeal process.

Meanwhile, I'd completed another quarter of school! My next visit to the doctor was promising. We continued to adjust my meds to ease some of the things I was going through. My sense of day and night was abnormal. All my life I'd been an early-riser, but since my shunt surgery I'd become a night owl. In some ways it was great, since Ken was a night owl, too. Yet something felt wrong about it, and it was hard to get to work on time in the morning. Some days I was so sleepy I was afraid of causing a driving accident. And with homework to do, I couldn't be using up my free time for naps.

Our 22nd wedding anniversary was coming up shortly. I'd just passed my first "shuntiversary", or anniversary of shunt surgery. Kaitlyn was graduating from eighth grade, Learning Works and her K-8 school. Easter, my favorite holiday, was on Sunday. Hallelujah!

Cel' e bra' tion: 1. a joyful occasion for special festivities to mark some happy event. 2. any joyous diversion. 3. To engage in festivities.

CHAPTER SEVEN

An Unexpected Portage

SOMETIMES, WHEN CANOEING in the Boundary Waters Canoe Area of northern Minnesota, someone reads the map wrong or there is unexpected flooding in an area or a boggy spot, making it necessary to portage. This may require some serious discussion and spontaneous planning to navigate a poorly defined trail to the next lake.

It was a rough week; the end of March. Justine was not following instructions or taking care of herself. Her memory was noticeably worse. Eventually, it became clear that it was time to plan for assistance with her. I was worrying too much about her living all by herself and my having to spend so much time at her house sorting through possessions. Even a person who writes to a different person every day of the year doesn't need as many greeting cards and stationery as she had stock-piled. It was incredible. Admittedly, I like stationery, too, but not *that* much.

My parents, who lived by themselves in the house I'd grown up in, were sick with the stomach flu. By the way, there is no such thing as the stomach flu. Flu is short for influenza, which has nothing to do with the stomach, but it is a commonly used expression. I volunteered to care for their Bichon frise, Mickey, at my house and brought them some groceries when I picked him up.

I began having regular headaches. The weather? MSG in my Chinese lunch? It took about 24 hours from the time I first felt a headache coming on to feel really normal again. It usually started with a feeling of extreme sleepiness and fullness in my head and sinuses. From there it progressed to pain, mostly on one side of my face and behind my eyes. My face became sore to the touch. My eyes were sensitive to light. Sometimes I became nauseated.

Conversing with others I'd met who have brain shunts for hydrocephalus, I found that most of them had headaches, too. Surgical placement of a ventriculoperitoneal shunt like mine is one of only a few treatments available, and hydrocephalus does not yet have a cure. My cerebrospinal fluid continues to be made by choroid plexus cells (this is good), even when the pressure in my head increases (this is bad). I tried everything I could think of to "deal with" the headaches and continue my life. Yoga, eating a healthier diet, caffeine.

I attempted to create a "normal" flow of life within my family. We acquired some gold fish for our aquarium. Gold fish can live twenty to thirty years in a perfect environment. They like to eat a lot. They are the Labrador retrievers of aquarium fish; they are hungry, energetic and poop a lot. Thus, they need partial water changes frequently and space to grow. We enjoyed their bright orange colors, flowing fins and tails, and graceful movements.

Kaitlyn needed my attention with normal teenage issues. By the end of April, when I had a headache it felt like my eyes wanted to cross by themselves. Justine needed a MRI; my mom, Marci, was scheduled for spinal fusion surgery mid-May. My dad, Bob, was becoming increasingly forgetful. Both Mom and Dad would need care during Mom's recovery. Heidi, one of our cats, needed another anesthetized dental cleaning. I was feeling my limitations.

Heidi's dental procedure went well. She didn't have many disintegrating teeth this time. Each time she had a dental procedure she became more affectionate and relaxed. Her mouth clearly had been hurting for longer than we had noticed.

Cour' age 1.The state or quality of mind or spirit that enables one to face danger, fear or vicissitudes with self-possession, confidence, and resolution; bravery.

May came. I made a difficult decision. To save my sanity and properly care for myself, I withdrew from my classes at school. Now I could focus on all the doctor and dental visits that we needed to go to. There would be many in the next couple of months.

A meeting with my brother and parents regarding Mom's surgery and rehabilitation went very well. Dad was beginning to realize how dependent he was on Mom. He refused to go to a facility with assisted living, however, so my brother and I had to figure out how we could check in on him frequently at his house.

I walked the Humane Society Walk For Animals with the staff of the vet clinic again that year. I was thankful for the opportunity to care for animals, and for Kaitlyn's growing and learning, and for Ken's loving care of his family, and for the words of the Bible, which I devoured hungrily.

On May 5th, we received word that our appeal to the school board had been accepted. Kaitlyn would be able to attend the school she wanted to. Her friends would be able to, as well. I nearly shouted for joy during the phone call with the Minneapolis Public Schools personnel!

Grate' ful: 1. Having a due sense of benefits received; kindly disposed toward one from whom a favor has been received; willing to acknowledge and repay, or give thanks for, benefits; as, a grateful heart. 2. Affording pleasure; pleasing to the senses.

I commented in my journal, "At my annual comprehensive neurosurgical shunt exam, we tweaked my pressure setting up ten milliliters. We will see if that does anything to help my headaches. Otherwise, my shunt and my brain look wonderful! Thanks to You, O Lord!"

Three days later, I worked the whole day, then brought my Saturn to the shop for a tune up and oil change. They also fixed my loose motor-mount. If only fixing living things were that easy! I stocked up on cat food in preparation for Mickey coming over that Tuesday, since I wouldn't have time to buy it then. I washed three loads of laundry and updated the family calendar. I was so used to constantly having too much to do, too much to think about and too much pressure (no pun intended). It was hard to slow down and relax.

A few days later, my alarm went off at 4:30 am, and after taking care of all the animals, including Mom's dog, Mickey, I drove the short distance to my parents' house to pick up Mom for her spinal fusion surgery. Dad had gotten up early to help Mom get ready but he'd forgotten I was coming and was thinking *he* was taking her to the hospital. I drove her; we arrived early. She was prepped for surgery. My brother met us there in pre-op and I passed the torch to him. We enjoyed breakfast in the hospital cafeteria and talked. He stayed at the hospital all day while I went to work.

Mom's surgery went well. My work day went well; my brother kept me informed via cell phone. Mom was in a lot of pain after the spinal fusion, but had access to medication, so she was doing well. Her healing process went smoothly, except that the doctors couldn't keep her blood pressure stable.

My dad, like many men in his generation, was dependent on his wife to help him accomplish daily tasks. He also would not admit his frailty. The next day, I spent three and a half hours with Dad and Mom and I thought I was going to die. My dad claimed, "I'm doing fine. I can do it myself." Yet he couldn't get in my car without grunting and groaning, due to his obesity and lack of exercise. He insisted on doing everything his way because it was familiar. He couldn't walk around his block with a wheeled walker without stopping three times for a ten-minute sit-down rest. I had to tell him everything several times because he either didn't hear me or he had forgotten that I'd already told him. When faced with a new microwave food he wouldn't read the directions on the package, but instead asked me how to prepare it. He wanted to put up a chain across the basement steps so he had something to hold on to if he lost his balance while hanging up his jacket on the hooks in the doorway. He refused to a.) close the basement door, and b.) find another place to hang his jackets. Though I loved my dad, his persistently stubborn and fearful behavior tried all of our patience.

Seven days after Mom's surgery, I awakened feeling quite relaxed and headache free. The sky was sunny and calm, and I thought it just might be a good day. At the clinic, just before my lunch break, I assisted one of the veterinarians with restraining two Ragdoll cats. Nita was in heat, moody and had notes on her chart that she may become fractious. She swatted at and hit the vet in the face. The vet decided to pursue an exam anyway; Nita flipped out and bit me while I was scruffing her, held on with her teeth and held on with at least two paws, using all of her claws. There was no inhibition in her bite. Dogs and cats are amazing. They can use as little or as much pressure in their bites as they desire, carefully controlling just how much damage they do. This is how they can kill their prey, and then turn around and discipline their cubs or kittens with the gentlest of mouth holds. Nita was not holding anything back. My right forearm was covered with puncture wounds from teeth and claws.

We flushed each individual wound with two powerful antiseptics, important because cats notoriously have copious amounts of bacteria on their teeth and claws, and these were puncture wounds, the equivalent of injecting the bacteria directly into my arm. By the time a doctor was able to see me in urgent care it was nearly three hours later, and my arm was swelling.

That evening, I took Dad out to Bloomington to the Minnesota Masonic Home for an introductory visit. Dad was a Mason, so we were hoping he'd be inspired to transfer himself to the home while we had Mom there for her recovery. It is a beautiful facility, with historic brick buildings located on vast grounds next to the Minnesota River. Deer, raccoon, fox, and geese are visible from the long, curving driveways. Dad enjoyed visiting...but he didn't want to live there. He was convinced he would pass away peacefully in his own house, but was not considering what it would take to meet his medical needs while he was there. His was not a trusting personality, so we knew he would likely not cooperate with a hired caregiver to care for him in his home.

My brother and I were now experiencing what Mom knew all along, the amount of time it took simply to provide transportation for Dad. He was rarely able to keep to a time schedule; he had become extraordinarily slow at everything. He insisted on driving, though his reaction time had slowed. A few days later, he fell while carrying in groceries and using his cane. A kind neighbor assisted him into the house with his groceries, then called my brother, who called me. We ventured over to Dad's place to check on him.

On roughly Day 19 of our Parental Hospitalization Plan, I decided that, all in all, it had gone well. Some of the catastrophic events I'd been dreading did not occur. Everything I did with Dad seemed to take three to six hours to accomplish. Shaving, showering and making it to the Masonic Home for dinner at 5:00 pm became shaving–no time for a shower-- dressing and arriving for dinner at 5:30. His visits with Mom consisted of staring at each other and occasionally making random comments. Each of his trips to the bathroom took fifteen to twenty minutes. Dad loved seeing the deer at the Home; he almost started crying. He had always cried easily, so I didn't know whether they were happy tears or sad ones. I'm sure he had no idea just how dependent he was on us.

Mickey was getting along well at our house. I enjoyed caring for him. One of our cats, Gretchen, decided very early on that she hated Mickey and wanted him out. She would seat herself right up next to the gate we had that kept Mickey in the kitchen, taunting him to come over to the gate. When he got within reach she'd take out her claws and bat him on the nose. She would hiss and growl if he got too close. Mickey, on the other hand, decided he was welcome in this house and defied her by barking. But he always backed down. At heart, Mickey was a coward with an annoyingly high pitched, frenetic bark.

Thirty-seven days after Mom's surgery, Mickey, now home with Mom and Dad, needed to be taken to the University of Minnesota Veterinary Hospital for a lithotripsy consultation. He had bladder stones that were probably painful and causing bleeding. Dogs and cats, descended from wild animals, are genetically wired to not show pain until they can't take it any longer. In the wild, if they show their vulnerability, another predator will take advantage of them. Therefore, if an animal is vulnerable enough to show pain, it must be pretty painful indeed. Mickey's lithotripsy at the end of July went well, and he had more spring in his step following the procedure. It was meaningful and satisfying to me to know a medical procedure had freed him from pain and discomfort.

I have always found cleaning and organizing to be somewhat therapeutic. That being said, I was finding that I was getting much more therapy than any one person should need! Both mom-in-law and my parents would be moving out soon and their possessions had to be significantly down-sized.

With two households of accumulated stuff either being taken to non-profit organizations or brought home to my house for further dispersal, the task was daunting. In the end, the dispersal process would take many years to complete. Too many other things in life were a higher priority!

In July, tension was increasing at work. The recent economic down turn was causing tension in businesses all over the country. My relationships with some of the veterinarians were becoming increasingly strained, as well. This was a roughly seven-vet practice, where many of them worked part-time, a challenging practice in which to work because we saw so many patients and employed so many veterinarians. An exemplary vet tech or vet assistant had to be able to accept and understand the personality and assistance style of each vet in order to help them in the most effective way. This was especially important when the animal was not cooperating with the procedure, since our goal was to thoroughly examine and diagnose each pet effectively and safely. After my manager had had discussions with some of the staff members, she and I had a tense discussion as well. We agreed that it would be best for me to no longer work there. I was not being fired, it was only that they were no longer able to accommodate scheduling me at all, due to a number of factors, including my school schedule and my need for frequent sick time off. It was a heart-breaking, but amiable good-bye, much better than being fired or "let go".

My self-esteem plummeted. I doubted that I was making wise decisions. What do I do now? Do I dare search for another clinic job? Do I continue school? How good am I at what I do? Would I ever find a fitting career? I felt hurt and confused. This was a healthcare field; why couldn't they be understanding with regard to my health, too?

Some rethinking of my life and goals was in order.

CHAPTER EIGHT

Lake Three: A Stormy Crossing

HAVING COMPLETED THE arduous portage, it's time to get in the canoe and set out paddling once more. Except if there is a storm on the horizon. Storms in the wilderness can be frightening, because a camper is at the mercy of the winds and waters. It is usually best to avoid crossing a stormy lake in a canoe. Depending on the size of the lake, waves can be high and currents difficult to paddle through. Lightning should definitely be avoided at all costs. Still, there are times when a crossing is necessary; in those times wise planning must be done to ensure safety.

Fu' ture: 1. The indefinite time yet to come; yet to be. 2. Something that will happen in time to come. 3. A prospective or expected condition.

I was wishing that I, like Albus Dumbledore of Harry Potter fame, had a pensieve in which to collect my thoughts and free my mind. Sometimes I had an abundance of thoughts and feelings, and they were so intertwined, it was difficult to journal them.

I was doubting myself, wondering if I'd made the right decisions with regard to school and employment. I had the strange sensation I was in a dream or nightmare. I had learned through all the previous events in my life that I had a built-in, Spirit-powered mechanism that kept me out of situations that I felt were emotionally unhealthy. I had definitely thought that my work situation was unhealthy for me at this time. I cleaned and re-organized my house.... No bright light bulbs suddenly came on in my mind, but cleaning made me feel better. It is something I have control over. Something I do well. I can see the results immediately. It freed me to ponder, ask God questions, and think about my future.

Early in August, I awakened late one day—around noon—and when I got up to use the bathroom I couldn't see properly. It felt like something was trying to make my eyes cross-eyed and they wouldn't stop moving and focus on any one thing. It also affected my balance. Though I could control them with effort, the effort made my eyes ache and they were sensitive to light. This had happened before, briefly, upon waking up, but on this day it persisted for five hours. I didn't dare walk anywhere or drive. I had no nausea, dizziness, lightheadedness, or headache.

Two days later I awakened nauseated, with a slight headache around my eyes. I slept all day to avoid the pain. I vomited. I tried ice packs on my eyes. I searched my mind for an answer. The next day I realized I'd been drinking less water than my usual sixty-four ounces per day, and I was needing to eat and eat all day to keep up my energy to compensate for my empty stomach.

At ten' tion: 1. the process whereby a person concentrates on some features of the environment to the exclusion of others. 2. the work of caring for or attending to someone or something. 3. a general interest that leads people to want to know more.

I prayed, "Okay, Heavenly Father, You've got my attention now! Where are we going with this???"

A couple of days later, for the second time that Summer we sent our only daughter away to have fun. The first time was to a horse-back riding camp in northern Minnesota. The second was to a cabin slumber party. That day I wrote: "As a mom it has always been my ultimate goal to nurture and train my daughter in the ways of the world and the Kingdom of God, so that some day she can set out on her own and become the woman she chooses to be.

"WHY THEN IS IT SO HARD FOR ME TO SEND HER OUT FOR A WEEKEND!??

"I am a pathetic scum—I envy her. I want to go to a cabin, too, and go swimming, kayaking, talking with girls, getting tan...I miss her company. She is, after all, charming, intelligent and compassionate. And I envy her in a new way: I want to start my life over and have it be hers so I can avoid aging parents, endless medical appointments, assisted living and job loss. Life just HAS to get better than this." Kaitlyn was having much more fun that summer than I was!

Ten days later, Kaitlyn was on day two of a trip to Florida accompanying friends of ours to a condo on the beach. They visited NASA and went snorkeling in a cold springs. Kaitlyn loved the fine sand on the beach and the lack of rocks or debris. She tried sea food for the first time. She was awed by some of the exhibits at NASA. She missed our cats. She and our friends had called us five times already.

Meanwhile, all the adults involved in our family and theirs were tracking Tropical Storm Fay. The Florida Keys had been evacuated, and authorities were considering upgrading it to a Category One Hurricane. Kaitlyn was at Daytona Beach.

At this point, I need to tell you a little about my husband, Ken. He is gifted at fixing things and putting things together, especially electronics. Shortly after we were first married, he started his own Search and Rescue business, which he operated along side having a full-time job. Every once in awhile he would need to suddenly leave us to go assist in searching for a lost person. His role in the search was usually either technical assistance—with sonar, radios or specialty telephones-- or search management--deciding how best to organize the search for the most effective outcome possible. This man's mind and body are and were on the alert for any situation that might need searchers, and natural disasters fall into that category. Plus, Kaitlyn was vacationing in Florida with an equine searcher. That's someone who searches for lost people while riding on a horse, not someone who searches for lost horses, although I suspect she probably has done that, too. This woman was likely very aware of protecting her family from Tropical Storm Fay. So, instead of having a "normal" vacation time, Kaitlyn spent part of it holed up in a condo waiting for a possible hurricane to strike, while her dad in Minnesota kept in contact with her, tracking the storm, and giving them updates. It was a little tense for us!

While my daughter was trying to enjoy a Florida vacation, I began the process of introducing Justine and my parents to the concept of assisted living. We went on tours of facilities, were courted by them with meals and presentations and had discussions with staff. On August 20th I wrote: "Wow. Four and a half hours again. This time it was taking Mom and Dad and Justine on a tour of a senior complex. A lot of discussion and a really good dinner, plus the usual getting-in-and-out-of-the-car-commotion and it's-time-once-again-to-go-to-the-bathroom breaks. I am absolutely impressed with a staff member's ability to patiently repeat her answers to our questions and address what Dad and Mom-in-Law didn't want to hear but needed to: you need help with your care and your children and neighbors can't give it to you for much longer. It is amazing how many times Dad can assert that he's independent and can take care of himself just fine, and then lean over and whisper to me

that his doctor just told him he might also now have Parkinson's Disease....
And we all must have told mom-in-law five times that selling her house is not
necessary before she begins moving into a Senior unit. She can begin moving
and try it out before she even begins to work at selling her house. Oh my! Love
can be so exhausting!"

Kaitlyn and our friends arrived safely home from Florida. She complained
that none of our family vacations are "normal". She was correct.

I was still having headaches and my eyes continued to feel cross-eyed. I
was finally able to see a doctor and have two MRI's of my brain and orbital
sockets performed. The orbital sockets are the depressions that the eyeballs
are anchored in by way of muscles. The doctor couldn't find anything wrong.
It was frustrating.

I was caring for our neighbor's multiple cats and Mickey and our own
pets through all of this. People paid me to care for their pets. I loved it. It was
satisfying and fun.

On August 30th, my body didn't want to wake up in the morning, and
when I did get up around noon I had vision problems again. My eyes kept
wanting to cross, but I had no headache.

The month of September was spent slowly moving Justine into a senior
apartment and out of her home of fifty years. In my heart, I cried out to God
repeatedly just to be able to make it through each day. The whole family
must be in agreement with this decision–Ken's two older brothers in lieu of

their dad, who had passed away years earlier—all their wives, and mom-in-law herself. One of the brothers was not sure we were doing the right thing, and Justine was confused and terrified, though we'd begun this process many months earlier. Yet, we had to act now. There were forms to sign, finances to budget, decisions regarding what will fit in her new apartment—and where to put what wouldn't fit. We repeated ourselves over and over again to her. Emptying her house, I've never seen so much stationery in my life! It gave me a boost of energy to know she was finally going to get some help!

Kaitlyn began attendance at her new high school; there were wrinkles to be ironed out, but she was happy about her choice. We were happy that she was happy.

In mid-September, Ken's sister-in-law had a stroke. This, of course, meant that Ken's brother would have his hands full caring for his wife, not having time to help us with Justine. My dad was refusing to be moved to assisted living, but my Mom was more than ready. I wrote: "My conversation with Mom today confirmed that I'm not blowing things out of proportion—Dad really is in his own little world. I can only do what I can do. The rest is up to God. Lord, I just pray for Your continuing guidance and I pray You would soften Dad's heart to follow your will. I pray for Your loving support of Justine and, especially, free her from worry. Embrace my sister-in-law in a hug of assurance right now."

For me, being unemployed was a blessing in the midst of this, because I didn't have to juggle a work schedule with other commitments. What a relief!

I wrote, "All this is not a good thing. Really. God doesn't want me to be having vision disturbances and headaches. God doesn't want Justine to feel sad because she's moving away from all her good memories to an unfamiliar place. God doesn't want me to feel angry about quitting my job. He wants me to know and believe that He will use all these experiences and feelings for good, in my life and in other people's lives. For real good–not just a fleeting good feeling or a quick smile, but for a genuine, deep, penetrating good that will bring change to the world. God never does anything superficially. Still, I wish I had much more faith right now."

Later in September, I had an electroencephalogram (EEG) performed at my neurologist's office. I almost overslept and missed it. I had all the vision disturbances that morning. The neurological technician glued little electrodes to my scalp. Then the machine recorded a graph of my brain activity. S/he may have done more than that, but I don't remember anything else about the EEG. I found out the results four days later. An abnormality in the EEG showed I was having tiny seizures in the portion of the brain behind my eyes, perhaps due to the presence of my ventriculoperitoneal shunt. I was given a prescription for anti-seizure medication and told to keep in touch with their office.

So, having prayed and planned as much as possible, I was able to successfully cross this storm-ridden lake without capsizing the canoe and losing all of our camping equipment. I was ready for a peaceful camp site in which to rest and relax my paddling muscles.

CHAPTER NINE

Lake Three Camp Site

LAKE THREE'S CAMP site was in disarray, damaged by the storm. Oops! On to the next portage. It would've been nice to rest a little first. WHO planned this trip, anyway?

CHAPTER TEN

The. Longest. Portage. Ever.

IT'S THOSE LONG portages that get you every time, especially if the previous lake was rough and you're already tired. Just be sure you're armed with mosquito repellent. The annoying insects can form miniature clouds along portage paths. Look at the bright side: you might even see some wildlife! Bats and birds ravenously consume mosquitoes. River otter, red squirrel, eastern chipmunk, red fox...hopefully not a black bear or a moose. Though moose are not predators or particularly aggressive, they are not very smart and often do strange things when provoked or frightened, causing innocent bystanders to be injured. So, whatever you do, don't try to interact with a mama moose and her offspring. Better to hide under your canoe!

On October 18th, 2008, I wrote: "It has been fifteen days since my surgery–two weeks. It feels like it's been a month or more because of all the symptoms I had before the surgery. It is strange to think that it's possible that all my headaches, vision disturbances, etc. were from my shunt not functioning properly. I may not even have 'migraines'. Medicine is so much trial and error, it seems. I'm still on anti-seizure medication, and it'll be quite awhile before we try to take me off of it."

Wait a minute! My last entry was on September 29th, and it spoke of a weekend of moving my mom-in-law into her assisted living apartment. She would be spending her first night there. Now we're talking about surgery on October 3rd? How did that happen? And what was the reason for the surgery?

I remember being exhausted and relieved after moving Justine in to her new assisted living apartment. Now someone else could help us take care of her. I remember that my husband and I returned home and I crawled into bed to sleep. According to my loving husband, I slept three days straight. Then, his worry took over and he brought me to the hospital emergency department. He helped me walk to the car, but I don't remember that. I don't remember sleeping three days. I don't remember arriving at the hospital. Nothing. Zilch. Nada. Not a stitch of memory.

What had happened? I pieced it together by inquiring of my doctors and family members. My ventriculoperitoneal shunt had malfunctioned. While in the hospital, a surgical inspection of my shunt was performed and it was found not functioning. Cerebrospinal fluid had built up in my ventricles, placing extreme pressure on my brain. My team externalized the end of my shunt so that the fluid could drain. It was a true emergency when I arrived at the hospital. I was placed in the neurological intensive care unit during my recovery, then moved to the regular neurology unit.

Ah, the fountain sculpture in the neurology unit. I did enjoy the sound of the flowing water in that fountain.

Statistics show there is a fifty percent failure rate of pediatric brain shunts during the first two years following placement. I don't know that there is any data on the failure of adult shunts, but I suspect the failure rate is similar. The first shunt was invented around 1950. There have been minor improvements made since then, including the invention of a programmable valve and an anti-siphon device that can be attached to the shunt to compensate for the siphon effect. This latter device is helpful when the patient experiences drainage complications when transitioning between lying down and standing. Gravity does effect our bodies, though we take it for granted. Research continues on other viable methods of improving shunt operation and even possible methods of reducing pressure on the brain without the use of a shunt.

After being discharged, I was re-admitted on October 22nd; as they suspected my shunt was infected by a pathogen. Using cultures of my CSF, they found I was infected with a bacteria known as Steptococcus B, a common bacteria, but it didn't belong in my spinal fluid. I had blood tests, CT scans, and cultures, from which a result may take several days. Time. It all takes time. Time is precious. I had tubing draining CSF through my shunt, and intravenous (IV) catheter tubing putting sodium chloride and antibiotics into me. One morning, all before 10:00 am, I had an IV failure, a shunt tubing failure, a clean-up session, breakfast, a visit from a dear friend who is also a neurology nurse (and now my sister-in-law—imagine that!), and three visits from physicians. I was supposed to get up and walk around frequently, since that speeds up healing, but I was not especially motivated to do so. Ken had a virus and was feeling miserable, my mom was having migraine headaches and hearing difficulties, and my mom-in-law was coping with medication issues in her new apartment. Honestly, I felt like Job, from the Old Testament of the Bible.

Job was considered an upright man, who was also very wealthy and had a large family. By Jewish standards, he was a model citizen, a righteous man. He lost everything he had, including his health, through no fault of his own, yet he still trusted in and worshiped God. Job's "friends" gathered around him and tried to help him figure out what he'd done wrong to deserve such horrible events in his life. They had good intentions, but they didn't really help. Our expression "the suffering of Job" or to "suffer like Job" comes from this story of faith in the midst of great suffering.

Ap pre' ci ate: 1. To recognize the quality, significance, or magnitude of. 2. To be fully aware of or sensitive to; realize. 3. To be thankful or show gratitude for. 4. To admire greatly; value.

I loved having visitors! I was struggling to keep a positive attitude, and visitors helped me keep my mind off of my difficulties. When you have a broken leg or a broken arm or a dislocated shoulder, you don't even think about other parts of your body. You think, "How am I going to walk?" or "How will I play piano?" When there is something wrong with your mind...everything is wrong. My family and friends would ask me what my plans for employment were, probably thinking it would help me to look forward to the future, or to just think about other things. How could I have plans for employment when I don't currently have plans for a "normal" life? My last five months had been filled with illness, pain, surgeries, more pain, helping my mom with her medical procedures, her pain, my mom-in-law's life changes and caring for my immediate family. Wow. Sometimes it is good to just look back and recount the days like that; it reminds us that there are beginnings and endings, and that struggles don't last forever. The Psalmists were wise beyond words. They knew this and recalled all of God's past deeds that they could think of. This helped them realize that there are beginnings and endings to their current struggles.

"Does she need more surgery?", the doctors asked themselves. I had multiple doctors visiting me daily, including an infectious disease doctor managing the treatment of my infection. I was having trouble just thinking straight; it was additionally confusing to have so many professionals coming in to speak with me. Each one, of course, needed to see me to really understand my condition. Being a physician is a lot more than scientific method and statistics; there is an art to it, an understanding of what makes people tick, what keeps their attitudes positive. Our bodies are amazing. The role of a doctor is, quite simply, to create an environment in which the body can heal itself.

I missed Ken and Kaitlyn and all our wonderful animal pets. I was waiting, and healing, waiting, and healing.

On October 23rd, I had begun to have a full-body tremor that appeared suddenly that day. With medication, it was reduced to just a tremor in my right arm. It was a terrifying experience. Suddenly, my whole body began shaking and twitching completely beyond my control. This was not a seizure, during which the patient is not conscious of it happening. I was very aware of it. With medication injected in my IV, if I consciously stopped my arm from moving, the shaking was confined to my tongue or jaw. The medication being used for this was a very strong drug usually used for more serious Parkinsonian tremors. A possible side effect is an increase in addictive behavior such as gambling, spending money, or taking risks. The tremor medication has been found to work better when given three times a day, so it's not an easy, once-a-day-pill. This tremor, of course, added more specialists to my lengthening list of doctors. To this day, I have a tremor in my tongue that has never gone away, though the rest of the tremors ceased gradually over several years of the drug.

Soon, the doctors began to discuss surgery to replace the existing shunt with a new one, and putting in a PICC line so I could be on continuous IV antibiotics for another 21 days after receiving the new shunt. I was given a PICC line on October 26th and antibiotics begun. A PICC line is a peripherally inserted central catheter placed using sterile procedure, to allow medications to be given through it away from the hospital. On the 28[th,] I had brain surgery to remove the first shunt and replace it with a new VP shunt, only this time on the left side of my brain. Surgeons generally try to avoid disturbing the left hemisphere of the brain, since that is where speech is centered and speech is so important to our quality of life. This is why my left side was used only as a second choice. Once I was home again, I continued using the PICC line to inject the antibiotic.

Around this time, one of my newer friends from church gave me a pair of pink and white boxing gloves as a symbol of the fight for health and that we are all in this together. She had recently been diagnosed with a benign brain tumor. I had all my friends sign the gloves. They remind me of how loved I am and that I am surrounded by friends who care.

Waiting and healing, waiting and healing. At home, it was healing for me to care for our pets daily, and prepare for my daughter's fifteenth birthday party. Kaitlyn usually preferred to design and manage her own birthday parties. I jumped in to help like a good mom should, but was often told, "No, Mom." Social events were definitely her forte. I got to do all the fun stuff, like vacuuming, de-cluttering, inserting extra leaves in the kitchen table. You know. The fun stuff! Ha!

Our three indoor adult cats, a calico named Gretchen, a tortoise-shell tabby named Heidi and a greyish brown tabby with a very small bit of white named Princess, each had her own distinct personality. Gretchen was the most powerful member of the household. Each of the cats knew that if she decided she wanted your dinner, well, then you just gave it to her or spitting and hissing would ensue. Princess was being mentored by Gretchen to assume her position of authority in the future. Heidi had the least power of all. I had to watch out for her to make sure she was permitted to eat her food freely. Each cat was carefully trained to eat her food in her designated spot in the house in order to keep the peace. Three meals a day (to prevent over-feeding by free-feeding) kept us busy and them in tip-top shape. Plus, Heidi and Princess had irritable bowel disorder, causing a tendency to vomit up their food (eeuw. Too much information.) so they were on selected protein diets. Their litter boxes filled up rapidly, as well, and required attention. Our three birds, Alec the cockatiel, and two parakeets that had been rescued from another home, required daily feeding and watering and clean up. The fish in our aquarium required feeding daily and monitoring their water carefully. A busy household, indeed, but I loved every minute of it. Even the clean up. Most of the time, that is.

Also around this time, Princess developed the endearing habit of finding an appropriate object (like one of my prayer shawls that were soft and fluffy) and settling down to knead. This was a detailed ritual. First, there was selection of just the right feeling material. Not just any material would do. Then, careful kneading in a circular pattern using her hind leg muscles as well as her front. This looked rather awkward, but she certainly enjoyed it. This phase would last about ten minutes. Lastly, her eyes would become only slits and she would blink frequently until she fell asleep with her paws tucked under her in the "meatloaf" position. Once she was lying down, she was there for a long time. Little would disturb her.

Some time in the course of all these admissions into and discharges out of the hospital, Heidi began to sleep curled around my shaved and scarred head every time I went to bed. I think she was empathizing with me, since she'd just had so many painful teeth removed in dental surgery. Or else my head just radiated heat better when shaved. I like to think it was the first reason. She has a wonderful purr. It is neither too loud nor too soft, and is very even and regular. I have read information on the internet saying that a cat's purr is healing and comforting, due to its frequency. Cats purr to comfort their kittens, to comfort themselves and will purr when very distressed, presumably to calm themselves. I have seen sick cats at the vet hospital go from being crazed, fearful animals to quiet, purring kitties in pain. In any case, I am grateful for Heidi's purr that brought healing and peace to my recovery.

I know in November and December there were a Thanksgiving and a Christmas family celebration, however I did not write about them in my journal. There is one very short entry on January 6th, 2009, then nothing until June 21st, but my medical records indicate I had a CT scan and an admission to the hospital in January. On February 23rd I had an MRI and five days later was admitted through the Emergency Department for another brain surgery, a ventriculostomy secondary to acute VP shunt malfunction. Following discharge from the hospital, I had speech and cognitive therapy for several weeks. Each time I had a revision or surgery, my handwriting would deteriorate, then slowly improve again. In order for me to be able to continue driving a motor vehicle, I had to be re-evaluated by a certified occupational therapist/driving instructor whose specialty is observing and instructing in the passenger seat of the car. My field of vision was monitored closely, as that had been affected by the infection. It took 10.5 months before I was allowed to drive again.

This entire series of events was extremely disconcerting and frightening for me and for my family. I had an overnight bag packed and ready for Ken to pick up and take with us every time we went to the hospital emergency department, just in case. The good news is that my career experience working in various hospitals made them very comfortable places for me to be. Unfortunately, my family did not have that same comforting feeling when they walked into a hospital. They were not as excited as I was about learning new medical information by experience. They worried about me and my husband fought the idea that I would die. We needed some hope.

Following a tough paddle and an arduous portage, a place to set up camp is a welcome sight.

CHAPTER ELEVEN

Lake Four Campsite

I T'S ALWAYS BEST to set up camp while there is still natural light outside. That way one can find the way to the toilet and locate some Large-Leaved Aster leaves to use as toilet paper. Next, assemble the tent, get a good hot supper cooking and have time to enjoy the stars before settling into a comfortable sleeping bag and getting a good night's sleep.

Throughout most of my life, I'd avoided learning to play piano. I'd played violin for about 15 years, dabbled in recorder and bowed psaltery, but avoided piano because it was too "ordinary". Plus, it required using one's hands and fingers in a "mirrored" sort of way, which I found difficult. I'd avoided learning to knit for the same reason, though I knew how to crochet and cross-stitch.

I now had a new brain. The old pressure on my ventricles was gone, the pressure I'd quietly lived with for 45 years, unknowingly. So, my curiosity overwhelmed me: would this change me in any way? Would I become a different person? Would I suddenly have new abilities previously unknown?

The answers to these questions were 1.) yes. I now didn't have to live with the symptoms of hydrocephalus, 2.) no. I would still have the same basic personality, and 3.) maybe. The doctors said it was unlikely, but I held out hope to discover new abilities. With this in mind, I taught myself to knit! And I took piano lessons. I experienced something I had never experienced before, a connection between my right and left hands, in my brain. I could actually feel the connection, and the more I knitted and tickled the ivory keys, the more coordinated I felt. Coincidentally, typing on the computer keyboard became a similar experience. I think these activities actually help my brain to function faster.

One of the things I worked on in speech and cognitive therapy was what Ken likes to call "increasing my clock speed". Being somewhat of a computer geek, my loving husband compared my brain to a computer. Just as a microprocessor has a clock rate or clock speed at which it executes instructions, my brain has what neuropsychologists call executive function. Something about my thinking and my speaking was not connected, there was a delay that was infuriating. Frequently I just couldn't get the words out of my mouth the way they were forming in my head. It made others with whom I was conversing think that I was actually thinking at a very slow speed.

I went to a website for the National Center for Learning Disabilities called Understood.org to get a better understanding of executive functions. If I thought of my brain as a complicated series of hamster wheels, there would be one head hamster whose job was to monitor all the other hamsters and their wheels, making sure they were running at the speed needed to accomplish a task. The head hamster's job was also to evaluate the present situation and employ new hamsters as needed. S/he knows exactly what motivates each of the hamsters to work harder or slow down. In other words, executive functioning involves words like purpose, conscious thought, orchestration, analysis, motivation, planning and paying attention.

Gardening does not require much speech, and turned out to be a way to express my love for the natural world and my knowledge of biology without the pressure of speaking--unless you talk to your plants. I prefer to think my plants simply understand me without a need for explanation of my actions. We embarked on a native adventure, that is, we stripped the gardens around the foundation of our house of any plants not native to central Minnesota. I replaced them with plants and shrubs native to central Minnesota. Some of my friends thought this meant just letting the weeds grow, but NO! That is not the same thing. For example, though buckthorn is common in Minnesota, it is not a native plant. Dandelions and white daisies are also not native. So, in my garden these are weeds to be removed. I also manage our gardens using sustainable practices, as few chemicals as possible, and try to plant species that will provide food for wildlife and places for them to raise their young.

We have noticed an increase in animal species in our neighborhood since doing this. We live in a thriving urban community, yet our yard is home to grey squirrels, red squirrels, chipmunks, shrews, voles, mice, raccoons, bats, birds of many kinds, many species of bees, wasps and butterflies and ants. We have wild native strawberries, wild cranberries and wild grapes. We have the satisfaction of knowing we are contributing in a positive way to decreasing global warming and species decline. Our gardens provide a refuge for pollinators, such as Monarch butterflies and bumblebees. It is very rewarding and satisfying to be part of the biodiversity solutions rather than contributing more to the problems.

Given the difficulty I was having with executive functioning, my husband helped me apply for Social Security Disability. Because it involved accurately assessing my cognitive skills, it wasn't a pleasant experience, nor was it easy, but in June I received a call from the U.S. Government saying I had qualified. This meant our daughter would also receive a monthly check. It brought us a bit of relief in the midst of all that had been happening to us.

At this point, I had mixed feelings about my life, and still do. Had I not fallen and hit my head, I might have been a certified vet tech by now...might have been. Can we ever really know what might have been? Do we know enough about every human being on the planet to understand how our actions all intertwine to create our world? Some people live their lives into their 70's and then experience symptoms similar to Alzheimer's Disease or Parkinson's Disease, discovering they have congenital compensated hydrocephalus that has decompensated due to the aging of the brain. In some ways, I considered it a gift that I was able to find this out while I was still young enough to appreciate the outcome of surgery. But...

How did I get hydrocephalus to begin with? Was I born with it or did it develop early in my infancy? From the time I was young, I'd had a sense that "something was wrong with me". Psychologists would say this could be the result of many different things, such as depression, family dysfunction, etc. Yet, I have always had the need to understand myself. That drive led me into the field of medicine and science. The day I was told I had hydrocephalus I experienced an immediate peace. That drive to figure myself out ceased. For me, the diagnosis explained so many things. Regardless of how I acquired hydrocephalus, I did nothing to deserve it, nor did my parents. No one was to blame.

Still, I felt a sense of failure and loss. Children born since 1960 with hydrocephalus grow up gradually coming to grips with the reality of living with it and living with a brain shunt. It is all they know. For them it is a challenging part of every day life. There are support groups available for parents, to assist them in raising their child. Those of us with decompensated congenital hydrocephalus experience a sort of death and re-birth after surgery. Parts of life as I had imagined it before diagnosis would be different now. Some of my plans would not work out after all. Some of my dreams would have to die or be re-directed. It would take time to let go of the past and begin again.

I had fully expected to have a career in the veterinary field, which would help pay for my hobby of having a house full of animals. Now I had the responsibility of caring for them until their death, providing them with veterinary care, or making the choice to find new homes for them. The latter was simply not an option for me. These were my comrades in life, family members. I would find a way to continue caring for my pets.

CHAPTER TWELVE

Putzing Around & Exploring Lake Four

EVERY BWCA TRIP is different. We try new camping gadgets. We try varying the itinerary. We try catching our food from a lake. We try using a makeshift sail and the wind to power our canoe. We try a "layover day", a day of relative relaxation, of just doing what we feel like doing while exploring the wilderness outside and inside of ourselves.

For our layover day, let's return to Understood.org and executive functioning. Knowing when it's time to ask for help or research more information, raising a hand and waiting patiently for my turn, planning out my work day, keeping track of time, and remembering deadlines are all the job of that executive head hamster. Multi-tasking and remembering a phone number while I walk over to the phone to dial it. Adjusting my work plan to compensate for some new piece of information, or reflecting on my progress. Using previously discussed information properly in a group discussion. All of these use executive functions.

Jesus is the only person I know of who can do all these things perfectly, but some of us have more problems than others with these tasks. I seemed to be able to do most of these things before my brain injury; apparently my brain had compensated for the significant effects of hydrocephalus. I also had the benefit of a mom who taught elementary special education. I'm sure she doesn't realize how much that helped me and my brother growing up. I do remember having to struggle with testing anxiety, and depression and anxiety during certain times of my menstrual cycle (our family knows some good PMS jokes). Some children born with hydrocephalus, though treated for it, continue to have learning disabilities related to executive functioning. By using learning strategies, they are able to overcome their disabilities. As part of my cognitive therapy, I was assessed as clearly having difficulties with certain tasks and given strategies to fall back on when I needed them,

I had trouble remembering what a person had just said, especially if they talked too fast. It was difficult to communicate details in an organized, sequential manner, as in telling a story. I had difficulty initiating activities or tasks independently. It was especially challenging to retain information while doing something with it, like remembering a phone number while dialing it. It was virtually impossible for me to juggle multiple details in working memory. Working memory is like your brain's Post-It note system; it involves remembering one thing while doing something else. Working memory is what I use when I plan a goal, then work on each step to achieve that goal, while keeping the goal in mind. Combine this with the depression and anxiety people with hydrocephalus often feel, and it's a recipe for disaster and failure. High anxiety is a demand on working memory, because it means the person has to deal with emotions in flux at the same time as any distractions, keeping your goal in mind and trying to prevent yourself from running out of the room, shouting with frustration and anger.

To further complicate things--this is what the Psalmist meant when he said in Psalm 139 we are *fearfully* and wonderfully made!-- there are at least two different kinds of working memory: verbal (auditory) working memory and visual-spatial working memory.

Some examples of the first are: silently repeating a phone number while dialing it, following a multi-step set of oral instructions, learning language, and comprehending language. I loved learning when I was in school. School was laid out in an orderly manner, learning things one step at a time. In college I loved learning deep and mysterious bits of knowledge, with no thought as to how I might apply them, because I enjoyed the learning process. Once I graduated with my Bachelor of Science degree in biology, I was suddenly at a complete loss as to how to apply all this knowledge. What do I do now, I asked myself?

Visual-spatial working memory allows a person to mentally visualize an object or a concept. It allows a person to look at a map and know where s/he is on the map, or to familiarize oneself with a new neighborhood or a new route to get to a destination.

I have found that I now use an interesting combination of these two types of working memory to accomplish my tasks. I used to be able to learn languages quickly and easily; now I can recall what I learned a long time ago more easily, but learning a new language is harder than it was before. My long-term memory has kicked in to help me when my short-term memory gets stuck.

There is also something called kinetic memory. Kinetic memory, or muscle memory helps a person to learn physical skills, like holding a pencil, playing a violin, playing piano, kicking a soccer ball or hitting a badminton birdie. I believe my kinetic memory has jumped in and helped me compensate for my weaknesses, also. Shortly after my brain injury, I discovered that if I memorized information using yoga movements or walking I was able to recall more easily.

Incidentally, music has the same effect for me. If I memorize something giving it a tune or melody, I am sometimes more easily able to recall it later.

This practice can also cause strange stares and whispered comments, which is why I don't usually use that technique in a grocery or hardware store.

My family is learning–slowly-- that they need only tell me if I am repeating something to them that I have already said. I used to become impatient with having to repeat things to others. Now it is very near and dear to my heart to patiently repeat as often as necessary. And I am much more tolerant when others accidentally tell me the same thing multiple times. I have become more tolerant of criticism and instruction.

I began to realize early after my brain injury that strategic learning is very hard work. I had to be careful not to overload myself, and it didn't take much to do that. I frequently felt anxious about what to do and how well I was doing it, performance anxiety, which is ironic when I think that nearly all of my life I have sung or played music in front of others.

Sometime in July of 2009, Princess suddenly began to have more digestive issues, including not being able to keep her food down. Medications were not helpful, so we resorted to endoscopy, which is, essentially, putting a long snake-like camera down her esophagus to see how it looked. The endoscopy proved to be negative for anything concerning. We tried a different medication and a change to hypoallergenic food.

On August 18th, I had my driving evaluation and passed!

Hap'pi ness 1. Good luck; good fortune; prosperity. 2. An agreeable feeling or condition of the soul arising from good fortune or propitious happening of any kind; the possession of those circumstances or that state of being which is attended enjoyment; the state of being happy.

Out look 1. A desire, longing, or strong inclination for a specific thing. 2. An expression of a desire, longing, or strong inclination. 3. Something desired or longed for.

We began wrapping up my speech, cognitive and occupational therapy. Two weeks of it had stretched into 10.5 months. My therapists became friends on the journey. On the last day of therapy, I wrote in my journal:

"Today was a nice family day. Kaitlyn came with me to change the oil in my car and get four new tires put on. While we were waiting we walked around and 'shopped'. She got her ears pierced a second time and we picked out earrings. We found a pet food store and looked at cat toys. Ken is very happy with our choice of new tires, including the price. It was a beautiful day–sunny, no rain–and we stopped to say hi to Grandma and drop off some mail for her. We took her to McDonald's for a shake, and she bought us flowers at the Wednesday flower sale at her living facility. It was a pleasant day."

My mom-in-law, Justine, was not easily adjusting to her new home. Though she was and has always been a friendly, pleasant, cheerful person, her dementia was causing her to have thoughts that went round and round inside her mind in circles. She couldn't remember where all her belongings had disappeared to. It was apparent her belongings were of the utmost importance to her in a sentimental way, and she couldn't remember to which relative she'd given which item during the moving process. She would call us and ask where is such-and-such? Even down to a spatula or a specific bowl. It was quite obsessive. Plus, she was quite convinced her move had "happened so fast" when we had spent months preparing her for it.

Meanwhile, my dad, who was quite overweight, was having episodes of needing help to get up from a sitting position...or from having fallen on the floor...and refusing to consider moving out of "**HIS HOUSE**", because "**he'd paid for it**". He wouldn't think about the welfare of his wife, who had had spinal surgery and couldn't lift him. I was beginning to think our "crazy" plan of moving Mom out first and leaving Dad to fend for himself might actually be the only plan that would work!

By my birthday in September, I was knitting prayer shawls for others and participating in the Prayer Shawl Ministry at our church. I was knitting a lot. I enjoyed working with a yarn made of viscose and wool that required soaking in hot water to shrink the strands once the scarf was complete, then soaking in a vinegar solution to set the dye. The result was a very plush yet tightly woven scarf that was soft like velvet. And the skeins came in the colors of red wines. It reminds me of the verse in the book of Mark where Jesus is talking about sewing a patch of unshrunk cloth on an old garment: "No one sews a patch of unshrunk cloth on an old garment. Otherwise, the new piece will pull away from the old, making the tear worse. And no one pours new wine into old wineskins. Otherwise, the wine will burst the skins, and both the wine and the wineskins will be ruined. No, they pour new wine into new wineskins." (Mark 2:21-22, NIV)

I was becoming a new wineskin, and Jesus was pouring new wine into me. As the healing of my brain continued day by day, my parents were going through the trials of aging and I was choosing the path of helping them. My brother and sisters-in-law and Ken's brothers were all going through difficulties of their own, and I was the only one without a regular, full-time job. What a change of heart from years ago, when it had been me who told all my friends, "I will never do that. My parents are on their own."

Having explored this little lake as thoroughly as we'd desired, it was time to proceed to the next portage. According to our map, it should be just around this island...over there on the left...

CHAPTER THIRTEEN

Short Portage to Lake Five & Enjoying The Lake

NOTHING COMPARES TO the combination of vigorous exercise and the quiet beauty of a coniferous forest, though sometimes on a canoeing trip a person can encounter some surprising discoveries. A loon nest. A family of red-breasted mergansers. Spotting a feeding moose off the port bow. A rainbow after a sun shower.

I was managing our household, albeit inefficiently. Our native plant gardens were coming along nicely. I made a three-ring-binder of all the native plant information and photos to help us identify and manage the gardens. There were four fish alive in the aquarium, but the two goldfish weren't looking very healthy. Both Heidi and Gretchen were getting anesthetized dental procedures done. They are sisters; I think their loss of teeth was a genetically acquired occurrence. Removing their painful teeth raised their quality of life immensely.

My now-15-year-old daughter was having trouble accepting the new me. This combined with the spiritual dryness I'd felt since my last episode in the hospital made me seek God even harder. Teenagers are not exactly known for their amazing patience, anyway, but my daughter was unable to understand my forgetfulness and frequent repetition in conversation.

One beautiful fall day, our very pregnant next door neighbor and I were having a discussion over the fence. I made the comment that here I had all these child-rearing skills that would go to waste now that Kaitlyn was almost 16 and we had only one child. Not that we weren't happy with one, but it seemed so wasteful to go through all that trial and error learning to raise just one child. We talked about her awkward work schedule, since she was a professional violinist and now becoming a first-time mom. Then she asked me if I wanted to babysit for her when her baby was born. Without hesitation, I said, "Yes!" (remember that new wine skin?)

Will was born the beginning of October, 2009. Thus began my new career being a neighborhood babysitter! It was like being a live-in nanny without actually living in! And they could call me on a moment's notice if necessary. They paid me for my work and were always respectful of my needs. What a privilege to be able to influence the next generation some more!

By my mom's birthday near the end of November, I had been working hard to persuade Dad that he needed to either move or agree to hiring nursing care in their home. We were all at our wit's end. Exhausted and frustrated we prayed for wisdom. And prayed. And prayed. Then one day, out of the blue, Dad called up my brother to tell him he'd agree to be put on a waiting list at one of our local facilities. He and Mom had found a place he would settle for. Hallelujah! Our relief was immense...yet, doubts nagged at me. Would he change his mind?

Kaitlyn's 16th birthday was held at an indoor skating rink with seven friends. There was Dairy Queen cake, pizza and a sleep over. There was a lot of laughing, giggling, game playing, and everyone seemed to have fun skating.

A few days later, Kaitlyn stayed home from school, feeling ill. We went to see the doctor for advice. My journal entry says: "And she [Kaitlyn] actually said she was glad I don't have a job so that I could be home with her today. Wow. We moms live for moments like that!"

Thanksgiving, Christmas and New Year's celebrations came and went without any hitches. Any period of time without a traumatic event was a gift and very much appreciated. Dad did change his mind a couple of times, but by January 11, 2010 we had moved Mom and Dad into their new assisted living complex in Bloomington. The move was efficiently organized and executed by my brother and his wife with help from friends and family. Another big relief to thank God for!

I was spending more and more time with Will while his mom taught private violin lessons. His mom was right there in the house, yet it was my job to care for him and allow her to focus on her students. What a challenging and fun task! I enjoyed listening to her and her students have their lessons; they reminded me of my violin lessons when I was in junior high and high school. I could no longer play violin because of pain in my neck and upper back, but I still enjoyed listening to others play. It seemed like the perfect job for me at that time, allowing me to care for Will while being available to my family as well. It was also flexible enough that I could do what I needed to do to care for myself. I still had frequent physician appointments, and we'd decided to try four more weeks of speech and cognitive therapy to increase my "clock speed". I could control just how much stress I exposed myself to each day, each week, by paying attention to how tired I was getting, saying no to some activities.

Occasionally, something would happen to reinforce how important my work and volunteer time were for others in my life. I was putting off going to the Post Office to mail two packages; I don't particularly enjoy mailing packages. I walked in the door of the Post Office. There immediately ahead of me in line was a bundled up woman with her well-wrapped baby in a stroller. She couldn't get the baby to stop crying. The clerk asked if anyone was ready to be helped, so I jumped in and said I was ready. As I turned to walk out the door, I recognized the woman with the baby – it was Will and his mom! I offered to help her with Will while she attended to her package. I thought she was going to cry, she was so happy to see me at that stressful moment. I realized later I had recognized Will's crying and his baby blanket long before I'd recognized his mom.

Speech therapy was not going well. I was supposed to be performing at eighty percent accuracy and speed on each exercise, but I was performing at fifty to sixty percent. I compensated by using email when I could, but I worked hard at all the therapy activities they gave me to do.

Normal family life continued around me: We had a fiftieth birthday party for Ken, Kaitlyn was involved in church activities and school, I was pet sitting and caring for our own pets. In March, Ken and his brothers helped their mom sign on the sale of her house. We worked hard to remove all her possessions and distribute them. We also worked hard to sort through all of my mom and dad's remaining possessions, distributing them as needed. Mom helped us with sorting, but we left Dad out of it. He would have argued over all of our decisions. His memory and coordination were becoming worse and worse. Dad had saved everything he could, so the house-emptying process took many months to complete, including trips to the city hazardous waste disposal facility. We found pesticides and other chemicals from way back in the 1970's.

By March 5th, I had "graduated" from my therapy sessions. Testing had shown that I'd improved in cognitive function, and that was the goal. I was to continue playing games and doing puzzles that stretch my brain. My family helped by playing games with me. Soon, we'd established family game nights.

Though basically fun, I found them embarrassing. My clock speed was still slow. It hadn't improved by much.

Signs of Spring were peeking up out of the once frozen ground. Buds, green leaves and bulbs were sprouting, snow melting.

One Monday in mid-March while lifting Will from the ground, I felt a searing pain shoot up my lower back. It didn't get better throughout the day. I made the mistake of helping a family member move some boxes of mom-in-law's possessions on Tuesday, so that by Wednesday I was in excruciating pain. An x-ray of my back showed no problems; medications and rest were prescribed, but the pain continued until it was necessary to do a CT scan of my spine. The results showed two herniated lumbar discs that the physician wanted to begin treating immediately. Our insurance company, thinking they knew better, wanted me to wait six weeks before beginning treatment. We went ahead with treatment, an epidural injection of cortisone in the affected lumbar space. A local anesthetic kept me from feeling any stinging needles. They used an x-ray machine and dye to guide where they inserted the needle. They carefully talked their way through the whole process and I could watch the procedure on a computer screen if I wanted to. I felt instant relief, between the anesthesia and the cortisone injection. Next, some physical therapy sessions to loosen up my back again.

Time. Everything takes time. Patience. Faith.

We still had two houses full of stuff to empty out. Really? Could things get any worse? Where do we put all this stuff? We had to make room in our home for some of the antiques and sentimental furniture...and boxes to store and look into later...

This was an especially difficult time for our family. For some families, saying goodbye to the home in which you grew up is not easy. Ken would have bought his mom's house and moved us there if circumstances had been different. There were lots of good memories in that house and yard. Ken's patience was being tried; not only was he having a hard time being patient with his mom's forgetfulness, but he was working all day in a job he didn't like and spending his off time working on his Search and Rescue business. For Ken, a perk of all this turned out to be first-hand experience with how men and women with dementia make decisions. Many lost people that searchers look for are men and women with dementia who walk away from their homes, thinking they are going to catch the bus to see Aunt Penelope or to get "back home" to their childhood property.

I, on the other hand, was happy to say goodbye to my childhood home. Growing up had been emotionally difficult for me. My dad and I had a roller-coaster relationship–good days and bad days. While I was in college, away from home in Bemidji, Minnesota, I went through a life-changing process of forgiving my dad for our arguments and misunderstandings. In starting over, I found I still did not agree with him much of the time, but I didn't have to. I could be me and be different. I didn't have to carry all the anger and resentment around with me, and Dad needed to take responsibility for his own personal pain and anger, regardless of its source in his life. Based on some of his comments to me, I now believe that a small part of my dad's frustration with me was because he could tell there was something wrong with my brain function, but couldn't put his finger on it, and resources for parents of children with hydrocephalus were minimal in the 1960's. Neither was Dad an especially patient person, and I really tried his patience; many of his daily comments were racist and misogynist, and I was undoubtedly very vocal in my disagreement with his views. My childhood home was filled with good and bad memories; I saved the good ones and said goodbye to the house.

One of the difficulties of having dementia is that somewhere inside the person's mind, he or she knows something is wrong. During one of our Easter dinner gatherings, Ken's mom asked about the table dishes and decor, "Should I recognize these?" Quite a few of the dishes on the table had been hers. Recovering from hydrocephalus surgeries, I, too, had had times when I didn't remember something, or remembered it but was corrected by Ken or Kaitlyn when I'd recalled the information incorrectly. I empathize with those having memory problems!

On April 5th–Ken's and my 24th anniversary–I wrote, "A person can do only so much cleaning and organizing before she turns into mush. I think the brain mush has arrived."

Ken's family decided to have a "Goodbye, House" ceremony, officiated by our pastor friend, Ruth, to ease the transition for Justine and the Anderson boys. We gathered at my husband's family home, talking about memories of childhood. Ruth tried to convey to Ken's mom that she'd already done a great job of passing memories down to her kids. Later that night, after we'd told her once again and she'd hopefully finally learned that it was to be her last time visiting the home she'd lived in for fifty years, she paused to select a few last things to bring to her apartment. She had no more space left in her apartment, so I used discretion and left the items where they were. We had already moved all the really important things.

Ken gave me a beautiful bouquet of a dozen yellow roses for our anniversary. Even with brain mush, I can enjoy flowers.

In the North Country, common Bunchberry blooms white and low to the ground in spring. If you look closely, you may see Spring Azure butterfly caterpillars being hosted by the bunchberry. On the edges of wet wooded areas, you might see the delicate white and yellow composite flowers of Flat-topped Aster on tall stalks hosting Pearl Crescent or Silvery Checkerspot butterfly caterpillars.

There are forty-two species of native orchids in Minnesota, including our state flower, the large pink and white Showy Lady's Slipper, and the smaller Spotted Coralroot orchid. Orchids are specialized plants that require their own fungus living on their roots to survive and even to germinate the tiny specks of seeds they produce. Coralroot has a leafless red stalk, six to twenty inches in height, with many flowers. Each flower has one white petal with purple spots on it. The plant lacks chlorophyll and the ability to make nutrients from sunlight, so it receives its nutrients from the fungus growing on its roots. Most of these beautiful plants take fifteen to twenty years to mature and flower. They are best viewed in the wild and are worth the wait to see them.

CHAPTER FOURTEEN

What Lake Is This, Again?

T IME IN THE Boundary Waters is irrelevant. You get up at dawn, and go to sleep at sunset. Unless you like camp fires and stargazing. The stars in the BWCA are magnificent; there are no city lights to dim them. In Genesis chapter fifteen, verse five, God brings Abram outside, in the middle-eastern desert, and says, "Look toward heaven and count the stars, if you are able to count them."

In history books, time is indicated by BCE (before the common era) and AD (Anno Domini–Latin for "in the year of our Lord"). I have often toyed with describing my life as "BBI" or "ABI"--before brain injury or after brain injury.

By the end of 2010, I had driven up north to visit friends, my first long-distance driving trip since brain surgery.

Life went on pretty much this way–Kaitlyn and I practiced driving, all of us visited Mom and Dad, sorted through a box, visited Justine, sorted through another box, cared for our neighbors' child, volunteered at church in various ways, cleaned out Dad's basement, chauffeured a teenager to her activities, supported Ken in his endeavors, took care of myself–through Spring of the next year with a not-so-quick break (no pun intended!) in mid-Winter of 2011, when I fell on the ice and broke my fibula, one of the lower leg bones. In a home full of boxes and animals running around close to the ground or flying, crutches lose their appeal after about a day. It was a crowded house.

I found this quote in a shopping catalog: "Life isn't about waiting for the storm to pass. It's about learning to dance in the rain." I have found that instead of asking, "God, why do I have to go through this?" it is far more helpful to ask, "God, what do you want me to learn from this?"

"For surely I know the plans I have for you, says the Lord, plans for your welfare and not for harm, to give you a future with hope." (Jeremiah 29:11)

Kaitlyn decided to join the badminton team at her high school, and turned out to be very good at the sport. She would frequently ask me to play with her; we'd play in our street, which is fairly quiet. It was good exercise for both of us and it helped to re-build my self-esteem and coordination, though without question, Kaitlyn was the better player.

Ken was spending quite a bit of time away from home, searching for missing persons. Kaitlyn and I missed him, but it was also an opportunity for

Kaitlyn to learn more about all of her dad's many skills and aptitudes. Whoever invented "Take Your Child To Work Day" knew how important it is for our children to learn from observing what we do. The activities of our families are our children's most important experiences. She was able to go with Ken to some of his searches and search training activities, even pretending to be a lost person a few times.

My child caring hours increased gradually. Another family in our neighborhood noticed I was caring for children in their own home and asked if I'd be able to help them, too. I really enjoyed going to the kids' homes to care for them for several reasons. First, the influence of family on children is so important and for kids to be able to play safely in their own house. Second, I enjoyed the change in household and location; it gave my life variety and kept my home reserved for myself and my family. Third, kids in my neighborhood have so many of their own toys to play with, I didn't need to set up a daycare center! And lastly, getting to know the children in our neighborhood was bringing all of the neighbors closer together.

Having been an elementary school teacher, my mom had spent hundreds of dollars of her own money to buy books for her school room. Between the books she bought for my brother and I, and the books she'd purchased for school, she practically had her own library. When she and Dad moved out of their home, I took charge of her books, distributing some of them to a children's hospital and the neighborhood "Little Free Libraries". The books that were special to me, I kept.

Okay, now that I have all these books, what do I do with them? I started my own neighborhood family library.

It was important for me to keep my brain active and stretching. I read books. I read books to kids aloud. At first, it was hard to sit still for more than a few minutes, but this proved helpful in caring for very young children; they couldn't sit still for more than a few minutes either! Over time I was able to direct my attention to reading for longer and longer periods of time. It took years to get back to my previous habits of reading quickly and to comprehend what I was reading. I just couldn't hurry the healing of my executive functions. They had to heal in their own time. Patience.

And then, aging tapped me on the shoulder, saying, "Pssst! You need reading glasses!"

Really? I began having yearly eye exams; it turned out that eye doctors can tell if there is an increase of pressure in the brain, as well as in our eyes.

I never stopped being active in church. Singing was keeping my brain healing; thank God that opportunities abound for singing and musical activities in church.

By this time, I'd gained a lot of weight, despite a daily walking routine. My family doctor hypothesized, trying to be helpful. I was sweating bullets whenever I did anything, definitely a new problem. All of my life I'd had trouble with not sweating enough and overheating. Now I couldn't do any activity without dripping all over! Was it medication related? Was it the changes my brain was experiencing now having a shunt? The temperature center and weight control center of the brain are in the area affected by my shunt and hydrocephalus. I was having to purchase used clothing at garage sales to accommodate my body's increasing size.

I had to control my weight or life was going to get more expensive.

When I felt like I was accomplishing little, or life was proceeding too slowly, I would remind myself that my greatest achievement has been to have a healthy, happy marriage and to be raising a healthy, happy daughter, who was going to graduate from high school soon. Wow. As we sorted through my mom's and dad's material possessions, we would find something that reminded us what my dad was like as a young man. He was impulsive, went along with the crowd, and was exceedingly persistent. In addition, we found evidence that Dad had experienced PTSD (Post-Traumatic Stress Disorder) while in the Naval Reserves during the Korean War. There was so much arguing and unrest in my family growing up that had to have been the result of PTSD. I could have gone on to repeat that scenario with my own family, but I chose not to. My brother, also, chose not to. We chose to not extend the dysfunction to another generation, as so often happens. Now I had the opportunity to prayerfully, positively influence other families as I cared for their children. It was a joy, and my child care families enjoyed employing me!

I began to see hummingbirds, bees and butterflies in our yard in the Spring, Summer and Fall. And an increasing variety of birds. Our bird feeders were well-visited by many species. The rodent and rabbit population increased, too. We have some mixed feelings about that, but that, too, was a joyful reward for all our hard work making our gardens native. I was unable to work full-time, but I kept busy doing things that I could easily decline to do if the need arose to care for myself, which I was having to be careful to do, or I wouldn't be able to care for anyone else.

Then, the Wednesday evening before Christmas Eve in December of 2010, I slipped on a patch of ice, landing in a position so that my right shin took all my weight. Another trip to the hospital emergency department! When someone falls and lands in the position I did, usually s/he has two fractures, the orthopedist told me, one closer to the knee and one at the ankle. I was blessed in that I had just one fracture near my right knee and my ankle was only sprained. The doctor checked and re-checked my ankle just to make sure. That meant I wouldn't need a pin surgically placed in my leg. Hallelujah!

Christmas celebrations proceeded mostly as usual, though I was quick to refuse to attend any event that forced me to be on icy surfaces. After Christmas, household chores began to get backed up. I did most of the animal care in our family quite efficiently, but I could do hardly any of it on crutches. I needed to be able to carry things and use my crutches at the same time—doesn't work! I recruited Kaitlyn and Ken to help with caring for the animals. Being on crutches during a particularly snowy winter is also quite an adventure. We'd had almost 20 inches of snow earlier in December. I had to slow myself down to prevent further injuries. The upside to this was that the snow was beautiful, fluffy snow, the reason I enjoy Minnesota winters so much. And I didn't have to shovel.

Rested and nourished with some camp meals, the plan calls for rising at dawn and tackling the next portage. Maybe we'll see a mat of Bearberry on the ground along this portage. The red berries are eaten by birds and bears. With oval-shaped leathery leaves on woody stems, we might have to dislodge some moss or leaf litter to find individual plants.

CHAPTER FIFTEEN

I Think I'm Getting This Portaging Thing Down Now

CANOEING AND PORTAGING in the clean air of the BWCA strengthen a person's muscles and coordination if done properly and consistently. Like weight lifting. Like physical therapy.

"Day Six of my confinement. I have cabin fever really badly. I'm supposed to be staying off of my leg, but that is nearly impossible. I have to get up to go to the bathroom and sometimes help Ken and Kaitlyn with the household chores, so I get up to do something, then lay back down with my leg elevated. I can feel my leg swell, then shrink [inside a plaster cast]. Very weird feeling.

"Kaitlyn proudly did all the laundry yesterday.

"Ken gave me a sheepskin for Christmas, just the right size to fit on a pillow. I've been sleeping on the couch and living in the living room. Princess has adopted the sheepskin as one of her kneading/sleeping stations. She's so definite about it. Without hesitation she jumps up to a 'station' and immediately begins sniffing around, then kneads for a good ten minutes, then curls up in a donut to sleep. She's very methodical and precise about it. Not just any spot can qualify as a kneading station. She likes certain textures. My loosely knit prayer shawls, Ken's polar fleece clothing, Woolfred the sheep puppet, and now my sheepskin. She'll go to sleep in other places, but not using the elaborate kneading ritual."

"Day Eight of my confinement.

"The sixth day of Christmas.

"Six more days until Epiphany.

"Four more days until I see the doctor again....Aaaaahhhhggg!"

Ken helped me do child care and helped keep Kaitlyn busy.

On Day Twelve of my confinement, the doctor pronounced my leg healing nicely with still only one break evident; I gave up my green cast for a purple one. My family was not "feeling the joy" of the holidays as much as usual; they were too busy doing my chores. Kaitlyn was bored and Ken was unemployed. His jobs in the computer industry seemed to end as quickly as they were begun. Don't get me wrong–he was a great employee, but the industry and the national economy were unstable. Companies had to find ways to tighten their financial belts. They were forgetting that employees are a company's greatest resource, thinking of them as an expense.

With my brain injury, no matter what I tried, the healing crept along at earthworm speeds. Even my leg seemed to heal faster. I was not an efficient worker, regardless of what I was doing. If a task had a five-step process the completion of it went something like this:

Review all steps.

Do Step One.

Go back to check and see what Steps Two and Three are.

Do Step Two.

Do Step Three.

Skip Step Four.

Get distracted by an interruption.

Do Step Five.

Find that Step Four was missed. Do Step Four.

Review all steps to confirm they were completed.

If I attempted to do two activities at once, you know, such as washing laundry and cleaning the bird cage, where you can put a load of laundry in the washer, do Steps One and Two of cleaning the cage, put the washer load in the dryer and put a new load in the washer, continue Steps Three and Four of cage cleaning, go back and take the dryer load out, put the washer load in the dryer, etc. I would inevitably forget something. I'd find it later on in the day. Or I'd completely forget I was doing the laundry at all, because it was in the basement and out of sight. Then something—a comment, or the need to go into the basement—would remind me that the laundry wasn't done yet. Can you imagine trying to hold down a "regular" job with that kind of memory? My self-esteem suffered, as well. With friends I could make light of it, but it was really embarrassing to not be able to do what I once could do: juggle two simple processes, with occasional interruptions along the way.

It was a good thing that I wasn't trying to continue on as a vet tech. The children I cared for were pretty forgiving about missing a step in a process— usually we adults are the ones reassuring them, "We all make mistakes! Let's try that again." However, a step missed or a mistake made on the surgery table or in an emergency with an animal could mean permanent injury or death. That was not something I wanted to risk.

When I first started caring for Will, I was only asked to work for a few hours at a time. Will was an easy baby to care for—he smiled a lot and he only cried when he really wanted something known. He had his fussy moments like any baby, but on the whole he was easy going. As my neighbors and I got to know each other better, our trust in each other deepened, and they hired me for longer hours. Just a few hours of "working" was exhausting for me, so I was careful. When a year had gone by and I was still proceeding forward, increasing my responsibilities, I knew that I was healing. Yet, day by day it was a slow process and some days were better than others.

There were other events going on in our lives that made this time more complicated. It seemed apparent that I was "experiencing peri-menopause", as they say. Menopause is the cessation of the menstrual cycle, the moment it stops occurring, but it isn't a neat, organized process. It happens gradually, and a woman's body changes in ways that effect mood, emotions, distractibility, and coordination. For me, it took several years until I was through it. It's a trying time for most women; neither do their partners and families enjoy it much!

Ken, in addition to attempting to handle all of mine and Kaitlyn's challenges, had challenges of his own with his day job and his Search and Rescue activities. We were all struggling, every member of our family, it seemed, including other members of Ken's family, who were going through Parkinson's Disease, heart disease, serious conditions of the digestive tract–we were all in and out of hospitals!

The Biblical Job scenario was looking like a pretty accurate metaphor.

So, back to my leg. On February 1st, my cast was removed. The break was healing well. Physical therapy began in mid-February. My sprained ankle hurt more without the cast. Will's family were understanding and patient.

My family, on the other hand, was having a hard time knowing how to handle my brain injury. *I* was having a hard time knowing how to handle *my* brain injury. There are no manuals to follow; we here in the United States have that *pioneer spirit* that says, "I can do it myself. I'll figure it out myself!" but when a person's executive functions are injured, that initiative is gone. There was no one to tell me what to do next. Physicians treat according to their specialties, but they don't all come together to discuss a particular patient's numerous conditions and how they might effect one another. I, the patient, was supposed to figure that out myself. With a brain injury.

I had so many questions no one could answer. How long can I stay on Disability? How is that decided? Who decides it, doctors or an institution? Or me? How will I know when I'm healed, whatever that means, exactly? Will I know it when it happens?

For many months–years--after my shunt infection and malfunction incidents, the only way I could make it through a day was to begin the day in prayer and meditation, then write down *everything* I was going to do that day, even down to the minute details. Get up (check). Wash up (check). Get dressed (check). Take meds (check). Feed myself (check). Feed all the animals (check, check, check...). Go to the bank. Go to the grocery store. Put away groceries. I lived off of lists and daily planners. They were my missing memory. If I needed to drive somewhere I'd not been to before, I sat down at the computer or a hard copy map to look up how to get there. Once, I tried to wing it to bring Kaitlyn where she needed to go in St. Paul; it took us an hour to get there, because my mind's picture of how the freeways intersected was inaccurate. I knew roughly where we were–really, I wasn't lost-- but wasn't quite sure how to get to where we needed to be. Kaitlyn was annoyed and worried about me.

I was thankful for being surrounded by loving family and friends, and the fellowship of Christian believers. Church, however, was not necessarily all bright, shiny and sunny all the time. Churches are filled with people, human beings who can be self-centered, selfish, thoughtless, and envious. In short, human beings who are less than perfect. That's why we go to church, to learn how to forgive. To learn how to love people who are tough to love. To learn how to love ourselves the way God Our Father loves us. I sang weekly in church with a group of musicians who loved to sing to God. We had our human difficulties, however, and during this time those challenges peaked. We were arguing, worrying, and problem solving weekly. Plus, the church's new building committee wanted to vote on whether or not to build additions to our church. Our administrative pastor retired and we hired a new one. As with any change in leadership, procedures and policies changed or were modified. The atmosphere within our congregation was stressful at a time that wasn't good for me. Yet, I was choosing to be involved; I could have quit at any time, but my heart was in it, and I was discovering that my heart was a little more reliable at this time than my mind was.

Our country's struggles with the economy were hard on churches, too. Our congregation voted no to the new building project. While some members were angry, others were relieved.

The world went on all around us. Spring, Summer and Fall road construction in Minnesota. Colds, viruses, sinus infections all around. All the usual stuff. Life goes on.

With relief we arrive at the next lake and anticipate adventure and discovery.

CHAPTER SIXTEEN

Lake Six: Paddling & Bird Watching

I HAVE LONG ENJOYED bird watching. I began doing it while a student at Bemidji State University in northern Minnesota. I'm not one of those obsessed birders who drive all over the country to add to their life list of birds identified. I'm more of an opportunistic birder, but moderately serious, nonetheless. In the BWCA, a person can see Bald Eagles, various species of woodpeckers, a variety of duck-ish waterfowl, and herons and egrets. They are incredibly diverse and beautiful. I would love to be able to fly like a bird–they are so graceful and skilled! Most of my BWCA journeys have been filled with a lot of observation of what was going on around me.

On a beautiful May day in 2011, flocks of migratory birds flying through the Twin Cities made a day-long stop directly in my front yard. They had spotted something I had missed: our boulevard maple tree was filled with insect larvae hatching out of their eggs and falling to the ground below. Apparently, it had happened quite quickly, or I would've noticed them crunching underneath my feet as I walked to the car (eeuuww). I stood in my front doorway and witnessed what seemed like hundreds of birds munching away contentedly on little cream-colored worms, some of them approaching the front steps and doorway to see if there were any stragglers there. I didn't even need binoculars! It was incredible and awesome! In addition to the usual house sparrows, American robins and common crows, I saw Blackburnian Warblers, a Swainson's Thrush, Tennesee warblers, American redstarts, evening grossbeaks, catbirds, yellow warblers, yellow-rumped Audubon's warblers, black and white warblers, chestnut-sided warblers, and ruby crowned kinglets. Wow. I mean, WOW. And I was home to see the spectacle.

I was home to see something else that week: my daughter "coming of age". I wrote:

"The house smelled like body mist and hair spray. The sounds of serious discussions and giggling came from my daughter's bedroom, where she and her girl friend were assembling themselves for the high school prom. I knocked on the door after receiving the all-clear to enter. My nostrils were struck with the strong smell of nail polish. My eyesight was struck by the beauty of these two teenage girls, their hair usually straight, now in ringlets and curls, their eyes glowing with anticipation. They carefully chose their make-up and supplies, picked up their high-heeled dress shoes and verbally went through a check list of everything needed for prom night and a sleepover at a third friend's house not very far away. No dates for these young women. They were going to the dance with a group of friends."

Next school year would be Kaitlyn's senior year. Ken and I were feeling a little sentimental. After all, she would be our first and our last daughter graduating from high school. Dads are protective of their daughters, and rightly so. I was thankful she had a healthy body and mind. Philip Yancey in Fearfully and Wonderfully Made writes, "A healthy body is a beautiful, singing harmony between the central nervous system and the tissues it controls. Yet in all this harmony every neuron must determine its own action based on the many impulses that come in. The microscopic computer in each nerve cell gauges my intentions, consults other muscles, analyzes hormones, energy availability and the inhibition of fatigue or pain, and fires a yes or no order to its muscle group." (page 213)

Hmmm. Kind of like being a teenager-soon-to-be-adult, having to determine her own actions, gauge her intentions, consult with her friends, determine the state of her hormones and energy availability, and fire a yes or no to her group of friends!

Our daughter's senior year was *filled*. Filled with classes; learning guitar, piano and handbells; keeping close to her friends; dating; applying for admission to colleges, visiting colleges. We, her parents, were her transportation to many of those events, so we were busy, too. Life was completely chaotic. Teenagers don't communicate any more effectively than nine-year-olds. They both tell their parents the day before they need to know something. Chaos prevailed.

Dr. Paul Brand and Philip Yancey write in <u>In His Image</u> (pp. 239-241):

"In the Genesis narrative, the concept 'image of God' appears at the consummation of all creation. At each stage of progress, Genesis notes punctiliously, God looks back on creation and pronounces it good. But creation still lacks a creature to contain God's own image. Only after all that preparation does God announce the culmination of life on earth: 'Let us make man in our image, in our likeness, and let them rule over the fish of the sea and the birds of the air, over the livestock, over all the earth, and over all the creatures that move along the ground' (1:26).

"Among all God's creatures, only humanity receives the image of God, and that quality separates us from all else. We possess what no other animal does; we are linked in our essence to God...

"And yet, *we* are made in the image of God. For us, the shell of skin and muscle and bones serves as a vessel, a repository for God's image. We can comprehend and even convey something of the Creator. Our cellular constructions of proteins arranged by DNA can become temples of the Holy Spirit. We are not 'mere mortals.' We are, all of us, immortals."

Well, I was not *feeling* very immortal. I had to be careful not to exhaust myself. Though I looked healthy on the outside, my brain was still healing, and I was on five medications for various conditions. I also was not sleeping well; I'd suddenly fall asleep while doing everyday things. It was beginning to worry me. I did not want to fall asleep while at the wheel of a car or while caring for someone's child!

Child care, pet sitting, helping Mom and Dad (Dad was falling frequently), working on their house so they could sell it, Ken's unemployment, selling Mom-in-Law's house, church activities, helping Kaitlyn to be a graduating senior...I could have just sat around and done nothing, but keeping busy was helping my brain heal—or so I thought.

I wrote: "Yesterday, we were so excited to find a very tiny, newly hatched Monarch caterpillar munching away on the bright orange butterfly weed in our garden. Immediately I began to consider what to do with it, because I've left them in the garden before, only to find them gone the next day, probably eaten. I mistakenly thought the tiny caterpillar's worst enemies would be birds, so I discussed with Ken how we could put chicken wire over the garden to keep the birds out. While we were discussing this, another predator discovered the yummy caterpillar—a wasp. I hesitated to swat at the wasp for fear of getting stung, and it was very persistent in getting to the caterpillar. In the end, it first fatally wounded the caterpillar, then came back and took it away. I was disappointed. Monarchs are having a tough time these days and I was looking forward to nurturing the little guy into adulthood, so it could be released safely.

Then I remembered that predators are part of life, just as tough times are a part of life for all of us. The wasp isn't hungry anymore. The parent butterfly probably laid hundreds of eggs—where are the rest? Did wasps eat them, too? Have I created a wasp smorgasbord?"

No matter how hard I tried, I still had nagging doubts. How could I have had hydrocephalus from birth and not known it? When would my shunt fail again? Are there warning signs I should be aware of? Increasingly, I was becoming aware of how amazing it was I'd graduated from both high school and college. Many people with hydrocephalus have learning disabilities, needing help to stay in school. How did I do it? I did have one incident lasting a couple of weeks during which I was too depressed to continue in my college courses, but I sought help and was able to go back to school.

Time for a boating parable from Brand and Yancey:

"The summer I sailed the coasts of Britain and France, I was responsible for guiding the boat into the treacherous harbor of St. Malo, notorious for centuries as a pirates' cove. Jagged rocks hidden just beneath the surface of the water make the harbor unnavigable, except through one narrow route. To follow that route, I had to rely on two sets of leading lights to the harbor. I would fix our course by lining up the first pair, sailing southeast until the next two lights lined up. Immediately I would turn sharply starboard and keep the second set of leading lights in line. Our boat rarely headed in the ultimate direction of the harbor, but zigzagged through a pattern required to avoid unseen obstacles. I concentrated solely on the lights before me, putting my trust in the one who knew the harbor well enough to mark off that route.

"Similarly, God does not ask that we figure out the reason for each change in our direction, or look on apparent obstacles with frustration. Rather, God wants us to accept the circumstances in our lives and respond in obedience and trust even when they appear confusing and contradictory. Events not under my control, such as the war and the slamming of doors by the bureaucracy, served to guide me by blocking my way. These, in turn, sent me back to the Holy Spirit for help in facing a new set of circumstances requiring new evaluation and new strategies.

"I take great comfort in the promise of Romans 8: 'Moreover we know that to those who love God, who are called according to his plan, everything that happens fits into a pattern for good' (v. 28 PHILLIPS). God does not promise only good things will happen; nor does the verse say all that happens is sent by God. I seek God's wisdom primarily to guide me through and around circumstances that happen to appear, moving always toward the fulfillment of his will. And I have confidence that the end result of all things will show a pattern for good. Obedience to the Spirit at every point ensures fulfillment of that promise.

"I am, after all, a mere cell in Christ's Body. It is the role of the Head to direct the other members and coordinate the actions for the whole church. What God asks of me is simple loyalty, a commitment to follow the messages of the Spirit in whatever form they come, in a way that builds up the whole Body." (From <u>In His Image</u>, pp. 456-457, by Dr. Paul Brand and Philip Yancey)

I was curious to see what non-profit organizations there were to which I could give a donation in honor of those with hydrocephalus. After some searching, I found that the Hydrocephalus Association was organizing a Walk in the Twin Cities area to raise donations. I didn't hesitate to volunteer. The Walk was going to be in September, so I began to raise funds.

By August, another neighborhood family was asking if I would help them with child care. Within walking distance from my home, this family was needing child care on an irregular schedule, like Will's family. I liked the variety of the unpredictable schedule and caring for the children in their own home, though my house was very close, so I could take the kids there to visit all of our animals and get anything I needed to help make our days more fun. I was able to find ways to juggle the two families' schedules to assist them both. It was fun and I felt I was providing them with an important service. They were very glad to have me help.

The Hydrocephalus Association Walk in September went well, and not only did we raise money for the organization, but I also met several people who became supportive and knowledgeable friends on my journey with hydrocephalus. We were inspired to start support groups for adults with hydrocephalus, and although the groups didn't continue after a couple of years, our friendships have remained. We continue to support and befriend other adults who are newly diagnosed. It is truly a joy.

By October, Dad was diagnosed with Parkinson's Disease and Meniere's Disease, the reasons for his frequent falls. We had some pretty serious discussions with the facility staff regarding Dad's frightening paranoid behavior, as well. Justine was also gradually losing more short-term memory. Ah, the perils of growing older. Dementia in any form is not easy to cope with, but I had a unique perspective: experience with brain injury. I could speak from experience to help my family cope with some aspects of our parents' failing minds.

We just kept focusing on the day-to-day, just kept on going. It was all we could do, but it was enough.

CHAPTER SEVENTEEN

The Bog

I
T SEEMS LIKE every canoeist has experienced portaging through a bog. Bogs are very old, very smelly, very acidic places where some of God's best natural work is done. Swamp Laurel, Bog Rosemary, Wild Calla Lily (a relative of Jack-in-the-Pulpit), Pitcher Plants, and Cranberries grow in bogs. Cranberries are yummy, but portaging through a bog is not fun at all. The ground is wet and spongy, characterized by decaying mosses that can form peat. It can also be marshy or swampy with deep mud. I had to throw away a pair of socks once that the stain and smell of putrid mud wouldn't wash out of.

Our next two years were like portaging through one big bog, complete with fruit, scruffy Jack pines (those trees with the pine cones that only open by fire!) and beautiful Tamaracks.

It began in January, 2012, when Kaitlyn came out of the shower one day, very upset and saying she'd lost part of her vision. Her left finger tips had gone numb. We opted for an Urgent Care visit, and before we'd gotten there, her whole left arm was tingly or numb, so we adjusted our course to the nearest emergency department. Since her condition was not life-threatening, four hours passed before she was seen by a medical resident. By the time she was seen, she had experienced tingling and numbness on her entire left side. Migraines were the probable diagnosis, but to be on the safe side, she had a thorough exam by two doctors and a CT scan of her head.

That scan was a tremendous blessing for us. Since being diagnosed with congenital decompensated hydrocephalus, I was concerned about whether she might have inherited it unknowingly from me. Inherited hydrocephalus is rare, but it exists, and certainly, undiagnosed congenital hydrocephalus exists, because I have it! Kaitlyn's CT scan looked completely normal. Hallelujah!

It didn't, however, explain the vision changes, tingling and numbness, so we had to just live with a "probable" diagnosis. I've noticed that is happening frequently in medicine these days. Mysterious viruses, unknown conditions. Medicine has a wonderful storehouse of knowledge, but our knowledge is imperfect. We still have a lot to learn. Thankfully, Kaitlyn's symptoms subsided quickly and her subsequent follow up physician appointments were uneventful.

Meanwhile, my primary physician performed a routine physical on me and suggested I see a cardiologist for my SVT's and have a screening colonoscopy done. The colonoscopy was lovely, and my colon was lovely, too, which left my frequent abdominal discomfort and need to run to the bathroom a mystery. The cardiologist exclaimed enthusiastically that he was sure he could eliminate the SVT's using a procedure I'd already had done, but had failed to stop the SVT's. I decided to continue with my medication and not try the procedure again.

Pet sitting and child care continued and was going well. I felt appreciated and valued in what I was doing. We found out the new pastor in our church was going to be a pastor we'd known fifteen years before and we were excited for his first Sunday in July. We had something positive to look forward to!

There were good days and disappointing days. One day, I wrote:

I am so imperfect and so flawed, O God, and I can't meet your standards or even my own.

"I know. That's why I sent my Son Jesus."

Really? It's that simple?

"Yup. I love you."

Really?

"Really."

Our childhood is the most significant time in our lives, especially from birth to six years old. I was reminded of this repeatedly while caring for children in precisely that age group. And while coping with my family and preparing their house to sell. Our childhood will follow us all the way into adulthood. As adults, we have the opportunity to sort through our childhoods and pick out the things we want to throw away, just like we were doing, sorting through my parents' "stuff". I realized that it must not have been easy for my family to cope with my frequent childhood headaches, my need for instruction to be a particular format that my dad couldn't figure out, and my turmoil when I went through puberty. All of those events could easily have been influenced by undiagnosed hydrocephalus. My frustration with my family softened. It was easier to forgive. It was easier to move on.

I was absolutely ecstatic that Kaitlyn was preparing a duet to be performed at church for a special event we were presenting. She was playing a piano piece she had taught herself with a violin student of similar age, who would be writing her own part to play along with Kaitlyn. Very creative, very inventive, and both young women were very talented. It turned out absolutely beautiful. I was so proud of them both. And I had babysat Will while the young violinist was being taught by Will's mother. I had reason to be even prouder. Yet, I knew that God gives the talent, not I. I was only watering or fertilizing. Kaitlyn was learning the art of musical collaboration, a skill she excels at, and performs in the most respectful and thoughtful way.

As was evident in my journals, I was not sleeping well at night, and having more and more trouble with falling asleep while writing or reading during the day. I wasn't sure which doctor I needed to see about this–I was seeing a different specialist for every part of my anatomy! And I had a medical background to fall back on. What did people do who had no medical training at all? Plus, it was expensive for all involved--me, the insurance company, the doctor, etc.--to see one specialist, only to have them refer me to a different one.

By this time I was 40 pounds over weight, as well, and no one knew why. I was exercising frequently, trying to continue walking daily, doing yoga, watching what I ate...What was happening to me?

Kaitlyns's high school graduation was approaching far too quickly. She attended prom in a stunning black and pink dress, her boyfriend wearing a pink tie to match. She and her friends had their photos taken by her boyfriend's mother, a photographer. Standing in a line, they were all handsome. Yes, I'm going to say it: Just yesterday she was a 4-pound, 4-ounce preemie baby girl, the first girl in two generations, filled with promise and potential. We never did know why my water broke so early. Perhaps the undiagnosed hydrocephalus effected my hormones in some way? Now she was an 18-year-old young woman fulfilling that potential and developing her talents.

I wrote: "God, You gave her to us to care for, but now it's time for us to give her back to You, to let her go so she can find out more about who she is. That is so hard. We've practiced this many times as we watched her go out to play by herself for the first time, walked her to the school bus her kindergarten year and said good bye as the bus drove away, watched her walk away with a new boyfriend, saw her organize and manage her senior year class load of extra-challenging courses...We've got lots of practice, but I suspect nothing really prepares a parent for graduation day and going off to college. Our little eaglet now has the most beautiful eagle wings, and she will be soaring over the horizon soon!

"Heavenly Father,

You guided me–however imperfectly I followed You at the time–when I chose my life direction. Now guide Kaitlyn–however imperfectly she follows You–as I know You have great things in mind for her. Help her to be conscientious in keeping track of her financial aid. And be by her side as she makes decisions and makes mistakes and makes great works of creativity.

Your humble child,

Les"

My life felt like a convoluted maze, with no map provided, only a Guide Who wasn't always very talkative. I was certainly keeping busy and productive, but something was going to have to give soon. Well, it did. Give, that is. Three days before Kaitlyn's graduation, Ken and I had a serious argument. We hadn't had any arguments in a long time. All the pressures were just too much to take. My husband was like a horse wearing blinders over his eyes, and a wolf standing right in front of him. He was completely surrounded by hunters with guns to save him from the wolf. Because of the blinders, he could see only the wolf. Ken was seeing our glass half-empty, with the water continually evaporating.

Ken also began to verbalize his concern for me. He said I'd changed, but he couldn't put his finger on what he meant by that.

Graduation weekend went very well, in the end, but it did have its snags. Ken's mom said she wasn't feeling well enough to come. My mom called and said she needed to take Dad to urgent care because he'd fallen two days ago. Our friends from out of town arrived later than expected and some wanted to attend the ceremony, some the dinner, etc. It became so complicated that both Ken and I drove around to pick up and drop off people, just so everyone could see Kaitlyn. Kaitlyn was happy, that was the important thing.

Kaitlyn's wonderful graduation party was in mid-June to accommodate everyone's schedules. Our next door neighbor gave us the use of her yard so we could put out yard games for people to play—croquet, ladder ball, badminton, and boce ball. Kaitlyn, her friends, and our family enjoyed playing all the games. She made some of the desserts herself and decorated a cake in orange and black, her high school colors, and 50 cupcakes in maroon and white, her college colors. We had plenty of food and fellowship. It was a great success! We used our new patio, constructed by Ken, who had felt it was something he just had to do—something with an immediate, visible result, that we could use. Something we could all look at and say proudly, "Ken made that! Didn't he do a nice job?"

The evening of her party, we received a phone call saying my beloved elderly Uncle had been failing and was hospitalized. He was dying, and there was nothing more medically that anyone could do. My brother, my mom, Ken and I all drove over to St. Paul to give comfort and to say goodbye to him. Mom's beloved brother, Uncle was special to many people. He'd been active in politics and was a writer who shared his talents by working with several prominent politicians. A kind and devoted man, he had five daughters, my cousins, whom my brother and I had played with while growing up. We all crowded into a tiny hospice room with their mom and some of their husbands. There was laughing, singing in Norwegian, telling tales of remembrances and insights, and tears, all the while making sure one member of the family was holding Uncle's hand. His pain medication made him sleepy, but he was able to hear and appreciate our conversation. There were all the practicalities of finding a place for his wife to sleep next to him, making sure he had no pain, checking on each other to ensure all the families' needs were met. These were some of the most loving expressions I have ever seen during someone's death. All were welcomed into the room, no matter how crowded it was. All were welcomed as family.

That night, I had trouble getting to sleep, but around 2:30 am I finally relaxed and dozed off. Later we were told that Uncle had died peacefully around 2:30 am. The world misses my uncle, but we know he is with us in our memories and he looks upon us from Heaven. Maybe he is writing speeches for the angels, taking lessons from Holy Spirit, Who writes the speeches for Jesus? Who knows?

When beautiful, sharing, caring and influential people die, it feels like there's a big hole in the fabric of life. It's not a nice, neat hole; it has little rips and tears and places where the horizontal threads are pulled. That's why my most important achievements are maintaining a healthy marriage and raising my daughter. I want her to be able to laugh, cry, contemplate and rejoice when her father dies. I want her to understand and feel how Ken fits into the fabric of her life.

June was an emotional month. After helping with a neighborhood garage sale, I was hoping July would be more regenerative, but life was reminding me it was still June: while out to dinner with an out-of-town friend, we received the call that Ken's brother with Parkinson's had fallen off his bicycle and was at the hospital emergency department with a fractured cervical vertebrae.

One of the joys of working with children under the age of six years old is experiencing their intellectual honesty. Their agendas are simple; they are open and honest about their thoughts and feelings. I learned at an early age that openness and honesty are important to me, in both expressing my own thoughts and feelings and others expressing themselves to me. As an adult I learned that in times of crisis it is important to be honest with myself and my loved ones.

So, here I am being painfully honest with you, dear reader. Oh, *!&*! I wanted to run away! Would the devastating events ever end? Where are You when I need You, God? Please, please, O God, help us now! Is this what it feels like to be a Jack pine in a forest fire?

Jack Pine is the smallest of our native pines, and the only Minnesota pine tree with short needles. The short-needled trees typically sold as Christmas trees are usually spruces and firs. Mature Jack pine seed cones are curved and sealed shut with resin, making them look like large grubs. The bark is usually grey or brown with scaly or flaky ridges. In favorable conditions (sandy soils and bright sunlight) they can grow up to 100 feet tall, but are usually shorter. One Jack growing in the BWCA had been aged at 243 years old as of 2008.

Jack pine seedlings need direct sunlight; they will not survive under a shaded forest canopy, so other pine species will take over. This is where fire fits in. Natural, periodic crown fires melt the resin that seals the cones. The mature trees may die in the fire, but soon after the fire passes, the unsealed cones release their seeds into the ashes. The new seeds grow quickly in the fertile soil created by the ash, and bright unimpeded sunlight. The result is a beautiful, pure stand of like-aged Jack pine that are free to grow well into maturity, unimpaired by other trees seeking sunlight.

Another sunlight seeking tree is the slender, scruffy-looking tamarack. Having tiny cones and needle tufts of fifteen to thirty-five needles, it is an easy tree to identify and often seen in coniferous bogs. Tamaracks are hardy, surviving temperatures as low as -75 degrees F. and as high as 100 degrees F., living over 300 years if undisturbed. Though mature tamaracks are not tolerant of fire, they are one of the first trees to colonize peat lands and areas disturbed by fire.

CHAPTER EIGHTEEN

What? More Bog? Who Made This Map, Anyway?!

THE MONTH OF July began with some very intense and interesting conversations with my neurologist. My family was becoming concerned about my behavior, so I asked Ken to accompany me to an appointment. He requested time alone to speak candidly with Dr. P, as I will call him here. I had no objection to that, since Ken is quite good at sharing objective observations with others. Afterward, he felt comfortable sharing with me more details of his conversation with the doctor. I think he was so relieved after talking with Dr. P that it opened up a stream of conversation between us that we hadn't had flowing for quite some time. It was, ironically, a really nice day of "us" time.

I was starting to have compulsions to have collections of things I liked, somewhat like a crow or a raven. It was a known side-effect of my anti-tremor medication. A related side-effect was to take more risks, to throw caution to the wind, so to speak. If I were a gambler, I would have become addicted to gambling. I was having serious trouble keeping my goal in mind while in a store to buy a few groceries, coming out with at least one extra item that "it just seemed like a good idea to buy at the time". "Oh, come on, let's just get one!" and I would override both my common sense and any objections from the person I was shopping with. Ken and Kaitlyn could see what was happening to me; I could not. To those outside of our family, it appeared that I was gaining back my confidence and was completely healed. I had taken on some leadership responsibilities at church that gave me almost no anxiety at all– because I was on the anti-tremor medication, which was originally marketed as an anti-depressant, but taken off the market because it was too strong. It also could produce instantaneous sleep episodes and problems sleeping at night. Bingo. That explained a lot of mine and my family's concerns. It was a little bit like learning I'd just spent the last three years on street drugs without knowing it. I was incredibly embarrassed. Not that we hadn't been warned of these possibilities; it was just so different actually experiencing them.

The decision was made to wean me off of the medication for a couple of reasons. First, the doctor wanted to determine the source of my tremor. Was it a result of Parkinson's Disease, my surgeries, or damage done to my brain from exposure to hydrocephalus for 45 years? Second, we needed to get me off of the drug so my family didn't become broke as a result of my spending habits!

My family also learned that in order to communicate effectively with me, they needed to approach conversations differently. Ken asked for advice from Dr. P and passed it on to Kaitlyn when the time was right. I learned that the pressure from my previous hydrocephalus had probably caused permanent damage to my brain's frontal lobe. Executive functions. Problem solving is one of those. Both Ken and Kaitlyn are great at problem solving. It comes naturally to them, so their conversations were conducted in a methodical, logical manner. They were incredibly frustrated with my attempts at conversation with them. I relayed far more details than they needed to hear to follow the conversation. My thinking process, by necessity, was not logical; it was rather convoluted, though I might come up with the same conclusion. I'd also noticed that though my thoughts might be speeding along, it took great effort to transfer these to speech, so I appeared to be *thinking* very slowly.

That shed light on why I suddenly felt compelled to use my computer keyboard to communicate with others. Thinking like a computer had *never* been easy for me. In the first years of our marriage, I'd nearly thrown our computer out a window I'd gotten so angry with ordinary daily use of a PC. Now, we talk about a particular App or program being "user friendly" or "intuitive" and I want to scream, "NOOOO..." Yet, I was beginning to really enjoy sitting down to my computer and having an email conversation with someone, because I could type my thoughts much more quickly than I could speak them. Now that *was* a *breakthrough* for technology!

Kaitlyn's application to a college she wanted to attend in St. Paul was accepted. We spent the Summer helping her adjust to her new job and prepare for college in the Fall. Having experienced living on a college campus myself, I encouraged her to do the same. I knew it would be an important and positive part of her life that she would appreciate years later. I remembered my enthusiasm for college life and envied her having the chance to strike out on this adventure. Parents were invited to attend orientations and meet other parents, so I was able to get my college "fix" by being with her on campus. It was great!

On Labor Day, I wrote:

"Yesterday was an incredible, heart-wrenching day. A sad-happy-excited-worried-jealous day. A walking-up-and-down-four-flights-of-stairs-with-heavy-boxes-and-bags-in-a-building-with-no-air-conditioning (90 degrees F.) kind of day. A making-her-bed-twice kind of day—once at home, then again in the school dorm room. A day of listening to speeches made by important people at the opening ceremonies of the Class of 2016. A day of remembering my own college years. A day of realizing hers will be different from mine—a different time in history, a different economic climate, differences between private and state universities, different family situations, a half-hour drive for Kaitlyn to get to St. Paul vs. my four-hour drive to Bemidji. I felt the same way

I did the day after she was born: my life had just changed, drastically. My life has a huge, empty hole in it where caring for Kaitlyn used to be. Our house feels too big."

I had worried that the Summer lull in child care needs in my neighborhood would extend into the Fall, but I needn't have worried. I was still very much in demand. Then, mid-September while leaving the house of one of my families, I fell down the last two steps out the back door and my ankle turned under me. I felt like an absolute clutz. It was the same ankle I'd sprained the year before; it swelled and clearly was sprained again. My other ankle began to swell. A trip to the ER confirmed two sprained ankles, just before the annual Hydrocephalus Association Walk. And I was supposed to be one of the Walk Kick-Off speakers!

I was also discovering that weaning off of the anti-tremor medication produced a little bit of withdrawal. Weaning gradually was supposed to lessen the withdrawal–and I'm sure it did, but I'm awfully glad we didn't try to discontinue it cold turkey. I would have made a terrible, overly sensitive drug addict; I was glad I'd never gotten into street drugs. The weaning process probably did not help me to be any more coordinated than usual, and may have contributed to my fall down the stairs. I would just have to be more careful, since weaning would take a few months to complete.

By mid-October, my ankles were healing and child care was going well. Life seemed to be looking up, until Mom started having cardiac problems. A few months before, she began having shortness of breath while walking her bichon, Mickey. Tests performed through her doctor's office were inconclusive, and she continued having symptoms. The physicians were puzzled. In the end, they opted for an angiogram. Using a radiopaque contrast dye, a cardiologist recorded the size, shape, and location of the heart and blood vessels. The cardiologist found four more arterial blockages; she already had some stents she'd had placed previously, but more stents would not do the trick this time. She was scheduled for quadruple bypass surgery in mid-October. Once again, I'd be spending lots of time in hospitals. It's a good thing I felt comfortable in them.

Every day I stopped in to her cardiac ICU room, visited for a few moments, then walked the hospital corridors or sat in a waiting room knitting, reading, chatting, or listening to other families who were also waiting. This hospital had a meditation sanctuary that was beautiful and peaceful. A prayer labyrinth, cushions to sit on for prayer, partitions to provide privacy, bookmarks with prayers on them, a gas fire place, a beautiful fountain with smooth rocks that could be handled, stained glass windows, and complete quiet away from the normal hospital sounds. A peaceful, warm and soothing place to knit, chat with other knitters or talk with my brother and sister-in-law. Mom progressed smoothly, while Mickey stayed at our house.

Unfortunately, Dad was falling apart. He was clearly dependent on Mom. He looked blankly at me when I told him to push his help button to prompt someone to help him with a task. He couldn't remember that Mom was in the hospital. He cried when he tried to talk about Mickey or Mom. His hearing came and went. He couldn't initiate seeking help, and he couldn't stand up by himself once he was sitting down. He couldn't think ahead to plan for his needs. He became fearfully obsessive about certain things. It was clear to the Assisted Living staff that he needed more attention than they could give him. He would have to be moved to a room with nursing care. Mom would need nursing care when she was discharged from the hospital, as well. This would mean moving both them and their belongings to different rooms in a different building on the campus.

We were so overwhelmed. Without Jesus, we would've been completely lost. I knew He walked beside us the whole way. We were able to trust that the One Who created Mom and Dad would be able to guide us in caring for them.

By October 27th, Mom was in a regular hospital room with a roommate. She began the day by going into atrial fibrillation, then passing out. She called us at 8:30 am to tell us what had happened, except she'd thought she'd had a seizure. She also thought everyone had gathered around her then abandoned her, leaving her alone, sitting in a chair. When we arrived at the hospital, I carefully asked the nurse what had really happened that morning. She confirmed what was true and not true. The pain medications were playing tricks on Mom's mind.

A cardiologist was following her case to observe her repeated episodes of atrial fibrillation. Atrial fibrillation, or A-fib as it's often called, is the most common cardiac dysrhythmia, and is marked by rapid, irregular electrical activity in the atria of the heart, causing a slowing of the flow of blood into the ventricles of the heart. This, in turn, may cause an increased risk of blood clots, which can move to other places in the body, including the brain. Stroke is a concern when coping with A-fib. Mom was nauseated and vomiting, as well. A rough day for her—and for us.

On many of these intense days, I would drive to the hospital, drive to my house to let Mickey out, go back to the hospital, go over to the Home to visit Dad, drive back to my house to care for all of our animals, then walk next door to care for Will. Kaitlyn would come home from college to visit her Grammy and her neighborhood friend Andrew, and to get her "cat fix". We drove her to and from St. Paul, in addition to all our other driving. The cats loved having Kaitlyn home. They took turns sleeping with her, lounging on the couch with her, and being carried around by her. These were moments of peace in the midst of the chaos.

Shortly after the day of Mom's A-fib episode, in the midst of her transfer to a Heart Health Unit where the staff could monitor her arrhythmias more closely, my brother took a phone call while standing next to me in the hospital room, then asked if any of us had an aspirin, saying he had to leave-- and walked away. The rest of us finished Mom's transfer and left the hospital so I could get home to babysit Will. At home, my brother's wife called me to ask if

I'd heard from him. I hadn't received a call from him. She went on to explain he had called her to tell her he was having chest pain, shortness of breath and *he was on his way to the emergency department.* It turned out to be a false alarm, but the staff did all the required tests just to make sure he didn't have a cardiac condition brewing.

Oh, and to top it all off, we caught a mouse in our house! Now, I enjoy all wildlife, but I don't generally welcome mice into my home. I searched the kitchen, found droppings inside the dishwasher (ugh!), droppings in the drawers and one of the towel drawers had a cute little mouse nest in it, made of cat fur, mouse fur, dust bunnies and towel fibers.

After about 10 days of this chaotic activity, I was TIRED. Exhausted. Spent.

Mom was finally moved to her facility's transitional care unit, tired but doing well. Ken and I participated in family activities at Kaitlyn's college, while still caring for all the animals (no more mice, though). Our cousins from my dad's side of the family were visiting Wisconsin, and having heard about Mom's hospitalization, drove over to Minnesota for an afternoon of seeing Mom and Dad at their facility. I was still having to be careful of my ankles, so the going was slow.

Dad needed to be moved to nursing care. Somewhere. Any where he would agree to.

It amazed me that in those several years, only twice did I reach a point where I didn't know what to do with myself. Boredom was fleeting, maybe even non-existent. By the grace of God, I was "blooming where I was planted", and I was staying mentally healthy. Sane. The energy to do that did not in any way come from me. It came from the Holy Spirit and my constant attitude of prayer. Everything that happened throughout the day was immediately given to God. He carried all of it. I relied on Him to remind me of things I needed to do when I couldn't write down my thoughts. And *He was absolutely faithful to answer my every prayer. No exceptions.*

Before we'd officially had the chance to move Dad to nursing care, he fell and was moved to the same transitional care unit Mom was in. Mom was moved back to the hospital after a week of nausea, shortness of breath and general weariness from pneumonia. Dad was convinced he was being coerced and was surrounded by conspiracy.

At that point, I think I would have joined a conspiracy, if there'd been one, or created my own, simply for my amusement. Real life was overwhelming!

In November, I wrote:

When will all this end? When will the economy improve? When will I be happy again?

The next day, I wrote: Well, I'm happy again. One down; two to go.

To my brother, I wrote in an email:

"Hey, I just want to tell you that watching you with Dad has been like watching God with us. God's love for us is so deep and so steadfast that up until the very end He keeps knocking on the doors of our hearts, hoping we will let Him in. But He's not manipulative or whiney or groveling about it. He stands firm in Who He is. He is both steadfastly loving and firm in His principles. And He meets each one of us right where we are, making sure we have heard His message. Then, the choice is up to us. Sadly, even in the face of all that love, some people still choose to not let Him in. Should Dad not cooperate with us, always remember that you have done your best and everything you could do to help him. Only God knows everything that is in Dad's mind and heart, and how it got put there. We can only do what we see fit to do and say to ourselves, "No matter what happens, you have 'succeeded' because you were faithful to God and trusted Him."

Dad was moved to a permanent private room in the long term care unit of the same facility. Some days he suspected Mom of sleeping with another man. Some days he was back in the Navy. Some days he was back on the family farm. The trick was to have enough of a conversation with him to determine where he was that day, then go along with him in the conversation. It was pointless to try to persuade him of reality. He would switch to the conspiracy theory, if I did that. He was pleasant and cooperative if I played a "role" in his imaginary story. He made our visits interesting.

CHAPTER NINETEEN

F (Fully) R (Rely) O (On) G (God)

I DON'T KNOW WHO came up with that acronym, but I've always liked it. There are lots of frogs in the Boundary Waters. In some cultures, people eat frogs. Not me. I usually brought my own food with me when I was canoeing. I've never been much of a fisher-woman, but I've heard fishing in the BWCA is phenomenal. The best part, of course, is cooking your fish over a camp stove and eating it under a dome of stars with someone you love, which could be your mate, your friends, or your dog. But to get to the next camp site we have to get through the rest of this bog, by paying close attention to our steps while focusing determinedly on our goal.

Each time we reduced the dosage of my anti-tremor medication I experienced mood swings, night time leg jitters, insomnia, nightmares and strange dreams. The first week of December, I went off the drug completely. It was a rough week. It was hard to let go of the "high" feeling of always being comfortable even in the midst of turmoil. But real life isn't anxiety-free. It has its ups and downs, its fears and annoyances, and sometimes failures. It was difficult and embarrassing to explain how I felt to my friends. As it turns out however, I have a lot of genuinely loving friends and family all of whom were very understanding and patient with me.

I don't know who wrote the following four quotes, but I like them! I found them in a catalog of t-shirts and knickknacks.

In the happy moments

praise God.

In the difficult moments

seek God.

In the quiet moments

trust God.

In every moment

thank God.

There is always always always something to be thankful for.

In this house

we do second chances,

we do grace, we do fun,

we do I'm sorrys, we do

forgiveness, we do hugs

we do family,

we do LOVE.

I was enjoying having Mickey at our house, particularly going on walks. Yet, Mickey was afraid of our cats, especially our calico, who hated him. Gretchen had no reason to hate Mickey, she just hated all dogs. When I dog sat at our house, I kept the dog gated in our kitchen and separate from the rest of the house. This gave the cats freedom in their own house and kept the peace. Gretchen liked to test that peace, though, by sitting directly in front of the gate, waiting for Mickey to come closer, then swatting at his nose with extended claws. Poor Mickey didn't realize that all he had to do was ignore her. They were persistent in their efforts to prove that each deserved the whole house to her or himself. Ultimately, however, I was the alpha in charge in my house, and that was that!

By mid-December, I wrote:

"Eight weeks ago, I was multi-tasking like a fiend. Babysitting, knitting, the cats were peaceful, raising money for the Hydrocephalus Association, keeping the house neat, busy with Praise Team responsibilities, looking forward to supporting Kaitlyn's school activities, and my health seemed fine. Then, chaos hit. Eight weeks of chaos. Now, my mom is struggling to recover from heart bypass complications, Dad is in a nursing home, babysitting demand has fallen to an all-time low, the cats are fighting with each other, I've almost lost contact with the Hydrocephalus Association, the house is a mess, Praise Team is really struggling, and I am going through withdrawal symptoms from a drug I didn't know was quite this dangerous."

Good morning...this is God.

Today I'll be handling all your problems.

...so sit back, relax, and

leave everything to me.

The new year finally arrived, and with it snow, which always makes me feel better. Snow is like God's grace. It falls, covering all the dirt, covering all the differences between houses and yards, making us all the same, leveling the playing field. That's how God loves us. We are, each one of us, one of His creations and He loves us all the same, unconditionally. His love was healing me and giving me strength and guidance.

I had a few weeks of holiday vacation free of child care and parent care; I felt somewhat rested. Mickey went to his home with Mom, who was improving steadily at her apartment. She was overjoyed to have Mickey back! I was overjoyed to have my house back! The cats weren't quite sure what was going on, they just knew that the dog didn't come back and that meant life was good.

Mid-January brought my first menstrual cycle in 13 months. It felt like a cruel joke. Then, I came down with influenza, you know, the nasty bug the Flu Shot is for? I didn't have a Flu Shot. Oops.

When we received the news that one of my cousins died of a heart attack, my heart sank. She was 55 years old, had been caring for my aunt and uncle at their Wisconsin home in the woods, and working as a chef at a local restaurant. Both of her parents had heart conditions, so it wasn't surprising that she did, too, but sudden death is never pleasant for the surviving loved ones. She was one of the cousins I'd grown up seeing frequently, and a niece of my uncle who had just passed away. I became sad and depressed. I listened to Graham Cooke videos and was bathed in God's love. Depression tries to bathe a person in negative thoughts and lies. I fought the lies with truth. I am God's beloved. Jesus is my big brother. Holy Spirit is my constant companion and friend. This is truth.

I kept looking back to the days I was on the anti-tremor med to try to make sense of them and put them in perspective. How we perceive everything around us originates in our brains. Whether a flower is blue or green. A happy day versus a depressed day. Feeling confident and secure versus timid and frightened. It truly was a time of God making all things work together for good in my life. As I looked back on it, I tried looking at that time as "when I was normal" or "when I felt like I fit in for the first time in my life" or "when everything just came together", but none of those explanations worked with the *facts* about the drug. The fact that it is a drug that takes away one's inhibitions and fears, and allows more risk-taking. The best I can come up with is that God took a circumstance that could have been disastrous, and turned it into an adventure in risk-taking in a good way. Not that I would recommend the drug to anyone–I wouldn't–but at least my risk-taking had been limited to non-destructive activities.

I finally embraced that if I follow God faithfully and have the support of His people in fellowship so that God can speak through them to teach me, whatever circumstances I go through, I will be able to give glory to God and all things will work together for good. God's goodness will prevail in me.

All well and good, but I was still confused about my body. Menopause or not? I was moody and angry, not motivated to do anything. Afraid I'd say something to hurt someone I love. It was tough. I was having asthma attacks that weren't actually asthma, but they frightened me enough I'd call the doctor or go to the ED. It didn't help that my experiences were out of my primary care physician's realm of experience, so her staff would tell me to go to the ED. Severe headache, nausea? "Go to the ED to make sure it's not your shunt malfunctioning, then come see me." ED visits are expensive, even with insurance coverage. Is it really necessary for me to have a CT scan and shunt x-rays every time I feel sick?

I had a complete physical the beginning of February, during which we addressed those issues. Blood tests confirmed I was indeed actually post-menopausal. I began taking a different anti-depressant. The good news was I could now focus on an activity for more than 20 minutes. I could read for an hour. I could practice piano non-stop for half an hour. I could sleep at night. I no longer fell asleep during the daytime. What a relief!

My thinking–that clock speed thing–was, however, s-l-o-w-e-r. Not shallower, just slower, and my ability to put thoughts into words was slower, as well. Several years later I learned that my difficulties with speech may be from having my brain shunt placed on my brain's left side. I was often stuck in mid-sentence finding the word I was looking for. Well-intentioned people tried to finish my sentences, but I stopped them, saying, "NO, that wasn't what I was going to say!"

Dad was staying in the long term nursing care unit in their facility, but my mom wanted to move to independent living apartments in the same facility. I set boundaries for myself with regard to how involved in their lives I needed to be:

I prefer to help when I have a clear plan to achieve the goal and I can follow the plan.

I prefer to move items over to the new apartment quickly.

I prefer to be told exactly where to put the items.

I prefer to NOT be family psychologist or intermediary.

I don't have to understand my family in order to treat them with love and respect.

It was, and is, not my job to analyze my family's behavior. Loving detachment. It's like what a nurse does in a hospital to keep his or her sanity while caring for others. My goal as a caregiver was simply to love. It was not to bring healing or stop aging or analyze the family dynamics. God will do those things. There is a time for those activities, but it was not now. Moving Mom was the goal. One step at a time. One day at a time.

On February 21, 2013, we attended Dad's first care conference since his move to long term care. Care conferences are the name given by the facility to short, regular meetings of facility staff with a resident's family, to discuss the resident's care and bring up any concerns that either the staff or the family might have. In spite of his increasing number of falls in the bathroom, the staff said he seemed quite happy there in his new setting. He waved to or saluted everyone he met in the hall, pulling himself along in his wheel chair, and was excitedly showing off his recent haircut and complete shave. They felt he was adjusting well to being there. We all had had the impression that he would continue to warm to his new apartment and the staff for at least a few more years (he was 87 years old). We had just finished moving Mom from the assisted living apartment she and Dad had lived in with Mickey to an independent living apartment in the building next door. We'd had to move out all of the items that were Dad's, either back to their house, which was not yet sold, or to Mom's new apartment, or to Dad's new apartment. We were all exhausted and ready to not move anyone anywhere for a long time!

So, it was a complete shock to everyone when, on February 22nd, my husband and I received a 5:30 am phone call from my brother, telling us that some time between 2:00 and 4:00 am Dad had died in his sleep. The staff organized a loving and simple bedside memorial service for us and them to participate in before his body was taken away to the funeral home.

This, of course changed my previous rather firm decision of having loving detachment. Dad's death, for me, was a relief. Many years earlier, I'd mourned the virtual loss of my dad, when I'd realized (with professional counseling) that he would likely never be the dad I wanted him to be. I had learned, over time, that I could love him and accept him for who he was, let go of any anger I'd felt toward him, and move forward with my life, keeping a respectful distance away from him, because our relationship was unhealthy for me. It centered around control, anger, and arguments, and I had since learned the joy of loving, healthy relationships. The process of arranging a memorial service for family and friends began another time of healing for my family, as we discussed our feelings with regard to Dad's sudden death, his temperament, and the mystery of where all his anger came from. These were deep and intense discussions, but what a relief to be able to speak freely. We don't know what caused his death, but it was common in his generation to die of cardiac complications caused by childhood rheumatic fever, and this was a viable possibility in Dad's case.

We did have some funny stories to tell, though. When my brother and I stepped into the elevator to go to Dad's room and clean out all of his belongings, my brother chuckled and said, "He's dead and I'm still moving more of his stuff!" When I carefully checked all of Dad's shirt pockets for gum or wrappers in his laundry to be washed, I thought I'd found everything Dad had put in them. Usually, he'd used every pocket he had for gum, gum wrappers, bits of candy, ballpoint pens, and business cards. Then I was transferring a load from the washer to the dryer and found soggy gum, soggy wrappers, soggy candy, and soggy tissue bits! I found that one of the jackets had a hidden inside pocket I'd missed. Stepping over to the dryer, I found more gum and candy in there! I had to use a special cleaner on the barrel of the dryer to get the gum off. I thought, "His spirit lives on!" and smiled a little.

That Sunday morning in church, I'd experienced an amazing thing. Love. First, our pastor and the congregation prayed for me and my family, and gave me many warm hugs and kind comments. Then, I was able to hold a six-day-old baby girl in my arms, who, just last Sunday had been in her mommy's tummy. She was trying to open her eyes. It was amazing. And a few weeks later, a baby girl was born in Will's family, too. That was an incredible blessing for all.

You know, God sees us in an amazing way. He sees us in our entirety. He clearly sees our weaknesses and faults at the same time as our gifts and talents and successes. Yet he loves us anyway. He carefully takes us just as we are and molds us into something much better. He shows us our faults and gently, lovingly shows us how we can overcome them and be better. Humility is all about letting God do those loving things in our lives. My perfect Heavenly Father taught me that. If your dad wasn't perfect (and no dad is), my Heavenly Father can show you what your dad couldn't.

We don't know what our dad believed about life-after-death. He never wanted to talk about it. We do know he was given many chances to hear about Jesus and God's saving grace, including one just a few days before his death. I know God's grace is boundless, and no life experience, no matter what it is, could keep God's grace from Dad. Only God knows what went on in Dad's mind. I am content with that. I have learned I can live peacefully with the unknown.

In the months that followed, we worked long and hard at getting Mom's house ready for selling. And what I learned through this is that God wasn't all about selling or re-building a house; God was about building our family. I was learning love and respect for the personalities that the Creator gave Mom and my brother. We all handle grief and change differently. I needed to learn patience.

I was continuing to have strange dreams early in the morning. Not nightmares, really, but strange, nonetheless. It occurred to me that my dreams may have been about grieving for my lost jobs. I was having stress dreams in past work settings. The odd thing was that while I held those jobs I didn't remember dreaming about them.

Tax time came and went; my husband and I were not in a good place financially, and it was frightening. I clung to I Kings 17: 14, which says, "For this is what the Lord, the God of Israel, says: 'The jar of flour will not be used up and the jug of oil will not run dry until the day the Lord gives rain on the land.'" The prophet Elijah was staying with a widow and her only son, who had hardly any food left. Elijah reassured her that God would provide for her needs and the needs of her son. God did. He was faithful.

In the last five years I'd suffered a lot of losses:

my health

my husband's job (twice)

my first veterinary job

my second veterinary job

my dream of a career as a vet tech

my cousin

my dad

my mom's health

my mom-in-law's health

my dog (she had died before all of this started)

I'm not whining, here, just stating the realization that I'd gone through a lot of loss. I guess I had reason to be angry, moody, and irritable! I began to realize, however, that the theme of my life had become death. I had even begun to think about my own death—not in a morbid way, but to prepare for it. I wanted to have my own will ready and to have our house ready, so that my daughter wouldn't have to go through this seemingly endless process of getting rid of material things. My dad hadn't prepared a will or discussed his death with our family. My mom, on the other hand, was ready. She had prepared.

In May we closed on the house I grew up in. It was bittersweet, both a relief and sad. It was the end of an era.

Then, in August, another close cousin was killed in a car accident on her way to work, by an impatient driver hurriedly weaving in and out of traffic. Her four sisters and their families were devastated, shocked and angry. Our family and all of her extended family were shocked and angry. I had logged many hours of playing with her in my growing up years. It simply was not fair that she should die now. The family all rallied around each other and talked and cried together. There were potlucks and comforting conversations. Minnesota Lutherans, you know, share potluck at almost any event. Her death would be felt for years to come.

I can't possibly go into detail with regard to all the events for the rest of that year. They would easily fill a mini-series or a TV drama. Ken and his rescue partner were presented with an award for Search and Rescue; his partner interviewed on the TV news, definitely a highlight for us. I was still volunteering with the Hydrocephalus Association. Global warming was more than just an idea; it was happening right here in Minnesota, changing the unfolding of the seasons before our eyes. I'd added another neighborhood family to my child care business. I was beginning to suspect I had food allergies. I'd had another sleep study done to further treat my sleep apnea. Numerous viruses and sinus infections were passed around. Mom had been hospitalized again with heart problems (an angiogram revealed another arterial blockage) that the physicians decided to treat with medications rather than surgery. I'd had another neuropsychiatric evaluation to determine how my hydrocephalus injuries were healing; I was slowly improving. My daughter went on her first backpacking trip to Colorado; it went well. Mom had invited me to accompany her to South Carolina to see her sister, brother-in-law and nephew; it was my first time traveling and flying since my brain surgeries, and my first trip to see Hilton Head Island, a wildlife watcher's dream. The trip went well.

I John 4:16 says, "And so we know and rely on the love God has for us." (NIV)

Yes, we do! I did not take any good thing for granted. No blessing was anything less than a miracle. Others might complain about the color of their new carpeting, or the cost of having their yard re-landscaped.

I was just happy to be alive.

"Go ahead. Arrange and rearrange the stones on top of your beloved's grave. Keep arranging those stones for as long as it hurts to do it, then stop, just before you really want to. Put the last stone on and walk away. Then light your candles to the living. Say your prayers for the living. Give your flowers to the living. Leave the stones where they are, but take your heart with you. Your heart is not a stone. True love demands that, like a bride with her bouquet, you toss your fragile glass heart into the waiting crowd of living hands and trust that they will catch it."

Taken from Here If You Need Me by Kate Braestrup,

a true story about the death of her state trooper husband,

and her life as a game warden service chaplain.

CHAPTER TWENTY

An Undiscovered Lake, A Clear Flowing Stream

THE END OF a canoe trip of this magnitude is bittersweet. Spending many days learning the flow of life in the wilderness changes a person. We realize once again that the important things in life are family, friends, food, shelter, sunshine, clean water, and clean air, then are thrust back into our work routines only to have the world insist we are wrong. "What about wealth? Prestige? Fame? Stop thinking so idealistically! " the world bluntly shouts at us. As we load up the car and head back to the Twin Cities, I plan. When will my next trip to canoe country be? What will I do differently next time? Is there any piece of equipment that needs to be repaired before the next trip? How can I apply what I've learned on this trip to my everyday life?

Recovery: 1. the act or an instance of recovering; specif., a) a regaining of something lost or stolen b) a return to health, consciousness, etc. c) a regaining of balance, control, composure, etc. d) a retrieval of a capsule, nose cone, etc. after a spaceflight or launch e) the removal of valuable substances from waste material, byproducts, etc. 2. (Sports) a return to a position of guard, readiness, etc. as after a lunge in fencing or a stroke in rowing 3. a process of attempting to change dysfunctional behavior, as by abstaining from an addictive substance.

For me, every one of these definitions applied to 2014-2015. I spent the next two years putting my life back together.

It was my impression that our brain shunts react more slowly or less sensitively than our healthy normal brains when adjusting to changes in the atmospheric pressure. I noticed my thought speed changed depending on the weather; I felt a little "dull" in my thinking on cloudy, rainy days. Not knowing precisely what was causing this dullness, I began using a sunshine-simulating light daily for about an hour each morning. For several years after my first shunt was placed, I kept track of the weather changes, specifically the barometric pressure. I found that any time the atmospheric pressure changed drastically or quickly, I was more likely to experience headache, discomfort or pressure inside my head. If the barometric pressure was relatively constant over several days, I felt more or less stable; if the pressure was gradually changing over several days, I felt uncomfortable, especially in the area around my shunt valve. If there was a sudden drop in pressure over a period of 24 hours, as when a storm front moves in, the crown of my head was mildly tender, though not as painful as the headaches I experienced before receiving a shunt. Brain shunts are better than they used to be, but they are not the perfect solution. I believe the infection in my first one delayed my healing significantly. Either from going 45 years with undiagnosed hydrocephalus or from the infection itself, I seem to have a permanent disability that keeps a few of my brain functions from catching up to the rest, though I have seen slight improvement with hard work and time. My experiences are rather tame, however, compared to what some people experience with hydrocephalus, especially those who also have other neurological conditions.

Unrelated to hydrocephalus, I learned I need to be gluten and dairy free, a long process of trial and error, but, oh, was it worth every minute. When I eat a healthy, high-protein diet of fruits and vegetables, meats, fish and poultry, rice, potatoes and corn products, varying the ingredients daily and staying completely away from dairy products, corn syrup and high fructose corn syrup, I am free from gastric distress. Interestingly enough, my gastroenterologist determined I did not have celiac disease and all of my gastroenterology tests were negative. I continued on the restricted diet nonetheless.

My strange dreams continued; I asked multiple professionals why I was having them and/or what did they mean? No one knew the answer. I finally decided the dreams were part of my sleep apnea. When I slept soundly, I didn't remember dreaming at all. So, I learned to ignore them.

It also became evident through trial and error that perhaps for the rest of my life I would need to follow a strict regimen of eating properly and often, speed-walking daily, taking my medications according to doctor's instructions, drinking 64 ounces of non-caffeinated liquids daily including lots of water, and monitoring my sleep habits. I did not have the option of giving up any one of these things or letting them slide, and they all seemed to heavily contribute to the healing of my brain, depression and anxiety. I continue this regimen even now.

Speaking of regimens, I am positively religious about using my daily planner. If I'd grown up using an i-phone type planner, that would probably be my method of choice. I have chosen not to use an i-phone, instead using an old-fashioned daily planner made of paper. I write notes to myself all the time, and more than once those notes have saved me embarrassment or heartache. Some day I will advance to using an i-phone, when I am ready.

Each year I notice my short-term memory and ability to multi-task improving by very small increments, yet there is a clear break in my life, a distinct change in my lifestyle and abilities of "before brain injury" compared to "after brain injury". I wince when I see professional football on camera; if only all the players knew just how fragile their brains are! I will not be able to go SCUBA diving with dolphins again, nor will I become a vet tech. I am not the same person I was ten years ago. Maybe my age is part of the cause—I am older now. What a blessing it would be to know exactly how my brain had compensated for hydrocephalus on its own early in my life! If only research could find a way to mimic the brain more closely for those of us with hydrocephalus!

Sometimes I forget and need to be reminded that it's not my job to make sure all the little pieces of the universe are working together smoothly. It's only my job to make sure my piece is working to the best of my ability. In 2015 and 2016, two of our three cats died of cancer, another life event I had no control over. The remaining kitty, Heidi, is living to a ripe old age. She was the cat who curled up around my head as I was recovering from brain surgery. I believe she is an angel from Heaven, sent to care for me. She has done so faithfully. We know she will die some day, too, but, after all, death is part of life and she will be ready. My mom was slowly, but definitely healing. Justine was slowly, but definitely declining, her dementia steadily progressing. She made two more moves to specialized care apartments. All we could do was keep her comfortable and safe, and try to find ways to stimulate her mind and body. Thankfully, she remained cheerful and positive almost right up until the end. She left us a wonderful legacy of happy memories to cherish.

I had a sort of Post-Traumatic Stress Disorder from experiencing so many life-changing events beyond my control, one after the other, for so many years. I was afraid to make any plans for the future, for fear something else bad would happen. It made me wonder about those children growing up in war-torn countries. Did they feel this way, too? I had to very patiently work through all the fear and anxiety.

Eventually, I began to feel that I needed something to look forward to, a goal, something I could work toward that would take longer than a day or a week, something fun.

Some time early in 2015, realizing that the next year would be mine and Ken's 30th wedding anniversary, I firmly resolved to celebrate it in a special way. Thus began our gradual, but steady preparations for a trip to Alaska in 2016. I tested the waters carefully. Did we have enough money for this expenditure? Was anyone else close to us going to die soon? Would my brain shunt function well at higher altitudes? Would a terrorist hijack our plane on the way there? As our plans developed, I began to accept that making these plans would never be in vain. Plans can be changed. Plans can be postponed. The process of plan-making was good exercise for my mind, though I had to do it in short increments since it was tiring. During my daily walks, I listened to recordings of Alaskan bird songs and calls, trying to familiarize myself with them. Again, good exercise for my mind. I knew it would not be possible for me to actually memorize each song. My goal was to be familiar enough with them that when we went to Alaska, I'd at least be able to remember that I'd heard a song before, so I could more quickly look up the birds in a bird identification book.

This would be the first time in ten years that Ken and I would take a long vacation together, and only the second time in our lives that we would take a two-week vacation together; the first was our honeymoon on the North Shore of Lake Superior.

On May 28, 2016, our plane touched down in Anchorage, Alaska at 8:30 pm. As we flew over the sunny glaciers of the Chugach Mountain range on the way in, I knew deep in my heart we'd made it. We'd made it through the most difficult ten years of our lives. I was about to have the vacation I'd always dreamed of.

Anchorage, Alaska is very much like Duluth, Minnesota; both are international port cities. Both cities are surrounded by environments that draw many tourists for skiing, boating, dog sledding, and surfing. Hey, I'm not kidding. Some people like to surf both the North Shore of Lake Superior and Turnagain Arm of Cook Inlet! Both areas have great places to buy outdoor gear and are surrounded by beautiful state and national parks. Anchorage is flatter, though, and surrounded by high mountains. While there, we stayed with good friends who'd invited us to spend some time with them. We made excursions out from there by car, train and boat.

We saw the peak of Mt. Denali (formerly McKinley) in the dazzling sun from the Alaska Railroad train car. We breathed the fresh, clean air of the Alaskan coniferous forests. I identified over 30 bird species I had never seen before, by sound and by sight, including varied thrushes, a highlight of the trip for me--and a source of amusement for my husband and friend, who teased me about my birding excitement. We saw moose, magpies, and ravens wherever we went, even in the city, and black bear, grizzly bear, porcupines and Arctic ground squirrels in the forested areas. Beluga whales, sea otters,

Steller sea lions, humpback whale, and Dall porpoises highlighted our travels in Turnagain Arm and Resurrection Bay. We saw Dall sheep and mountain goats high on the mountain peaks. While in Denali National Park, we interrupted a family group of Dall sheep crossing the road and were entertained by a lamb's cavorting, playing with its mom and aunties. There was tundra and taiga, and temperate rain forest with temperatures of 0 to 60 degrees Fahrenheit, plus miles and miles of grasslands.

We visited Wasilla to see the Iditarod Headquarters, and held dog-sled puppies that were so tired and comfortable they fell asleep in our arms. Our friends are long-time volunteers with the Iditarod, so we got lots of info from them about what it's like to be part of the race. The Iditarod commemorates the amazing journey of mushers in 1925 to transport diphtheria serum from Seward (where it arrived by boat) to Nome. Mushers relayed the serum by dog sled from rest stop to rest stop across the state until it arrived in Nome, saving hundreds of lives. Today, the Iditarod race is around 1,049 miles long: 1,000 miles of mushing distance and 49 for Alaska being the 49th state in the union. The race celebrates the unique pioneer "survivor spirit" that Alaska is famous for. The race is not officially over until the last sled has passed the finish line in Nome and that can take 11-15 days or more. All the dogs are scrupulously cared for by veterinarians, microchipped and monitored throughout the race. All racers are monitored and tracked by volunteers at checkpoints.

Mushing is an expensive sport; dogs, sleds, many pounds of high-calorie food, breeding the dogs, veterinary care for each individual...all of it costs money. To just enter the Iditarod race is around $4,000. The race is supported by state and local governments, and lots of volunteers. Finishers get a nice sum of money as a prize, and there's first prize, of course, but all that money goes right back into the costs of the sport. These athletic canines LOVE mushing and live to do it.

Besides being able to spend this time with my husband of 30 years, the best part of the trip was traveling up and down in altitude without getting altitude sickness for the first time in 54 years of traveling, thanks in part to my ventriculoperitoneal shunt. My previous experiences with high altitudes produced a great deal of nausea and vomiting. Not everyone who experiences altitude sickness has hydrocephalus, but certainly the increased cranial pressure caused by hydrocephalus would make it more difficult to acclimate to higher altitudes, where the air has a lower barometric pressure. My shunt performed to expectations. I was able to freely enjoy the mountainous beauty of Alaska!

I was also able to write the last page of the final chapter in this portion of my life. Not that nothing challenging was ever going to happen to us again. Yet, as our plane touched down at the Minneapolis-St. Paul International Airport, I had a strong sense that as my life continues, I will be closely accompanied by the love of my Heavenly Father.

"What then are we to say about these things? If God is for us, who is against us? He who did not withhold his own Son, but gave him up for all of us, will he not with him also give us everything else?... in all these things we are more than conquerors through him who loved us. For I am convinced that neither death, nor life, nor angels, nor rulers, nor things present, nor things to come, nor powers, nor height, nor depth, nor anything else in all creation, will be able to separate us from the love of God in Christ Jesus our Lord." --Romans 8:31, 32, 37-39 (NIV)

CHAPTER TWENTY-ONE

The Kitchen & A New Diagnosis

IT IS THE summer of 2016, and we are going to rearrange the kitchen, together, my daughter and I. It will not be easy. I have to sort through thirty years of kitchen-organizing ideas in my head. I have always disliked cooking because I am not adept at it. I am a methodical, one-step-at-a-time person who fights something akin to ADD in my thinking. That means I burn things by becoming distracted while I cook. It means that the directions, "While the chicken is sauteing in butter, mix the flour, salt and spices together in a large bowl" are a recipe for danger for me. I will become distracted by the colors in the large bowl and how they remind me of...and take too long to mix the dry ingredients, forgetting about the chicken on the stove behind me, and...

It is a rare day when my mind all works together properly to cook something well and efficiently.

My daughter can't relate to that because from birth she has been able to multi-task better than most. She learned to play a drum set at an early age. She taught herself piano. She often plays complicated board games that require her mind to process many things at once, just for fun. Playing a complicated board game for me is a mental challenge, like going to the next level of crossword puzzles. Sometimes it's fun, but more often it's a struggle. For my daughter, it is a chance to challenge her mind, to see what else she can do, and how well and how fast she can do it.

When she was in high school, a time when most young girls are forming themselves, becoming adults, and having the urge to step out on their own, our family was dealing with a lot of emotional upheaval—deaths, births, life-changing surgeries—which she handled by swallowing her pain and moving forward. She had to. Her mom had a brain injury and her dad was struggling with loss of jobs and his personal identity. I'm sure she felt alone, though we tried very hard to meet her needs. It was hard for all of us.

So, now, whether we all want it or not, while she lives with us post-college graduation, she is wanting to do all those things healthy moms and daughters do in high school, like rearranging the house to suit *her* needs. It's important for all of us to go through it together. It is healing for all of us, but not easy.

I'm crying as I write this and I'm not even sure why, but they are good tears. I think they are from a host of emotions: anger, loss, pain, pride in what and who my daughter has become and will become, thankfulness that, in spite of our uncontrollable circumstances and our weaknesses, she turned out just fine. She is resilient.

So are we, her parents.

Life continues on. Just last week in February of 2017, I awakened on Tuesday morning with a cloudy spot on my left eye that wouldn't rub away. It remained there all day and through our Praise Team gig at the Feed My Starving Children Mega Pack. By Wednesday morning, it had progressed to a headache as well.

One of the frustrating things about having hydrocephalus is diagnosing *other* conditions with similar symptoms. Fearing a shunt malfunction, I made an appointment with an optometrist to check my eye. He examined both of my eyes, inside and out–literally--and found my optic nerve to be inflamed. He was concerned enough about this that he asked me for the phone number of my neurologist, and attempted to call him. Dr. P. was unreachable, which I discovered by driving over to his clinic office. It was on my way home, anyway. I left another message with an administrative employee, who would pass it on to the neurologist on call for the day. I continued home with my cell phone at the ready. I never go anywhere without my cell and identification indicating I have a ventriculoperitoneal shunt for hydrocephalus.

Upon arriving at my house, I found my husband home from work. By this time, it was beginning to sink in that there may be something serious going on in my brain, and I was frightened. I answered my cell when the neurologists' office called to say they wanted me to immediately go to the emergency department. Explaining the situation to Ken, I began to pack a small bag in case I was asked to stay overnight in the hospital. This sequence of events has occurred many times since I was diagnosed and shunted for hydrocephalus. Due to full and unyielding clinic schedules, doctors readily send me to the ED, where there is easy access to full radiology services. The doctors check my shunt first, to rule out shunt malfunction. They look on the radiographs for kinks or breaks in my shunt tubing, and check the size of my ventricles for signs of recurring hydrocephalus. If all of those items are normal or in working order, they move on to the next diagnosis "rule out".

Ken knew that a visit meant he'd not be able to accomplish the list of after-work-action-items he'd planned. There are no quick visits to the emergency department.

This particular ED visit was an especially long one. We rolled into the hospital driveway around 5:30 pm and didn't leave until 11:30 pm. Ken sat beside me through all of it, calling our daughter who now lives a few blocks away from our house, to ask her to check on our cat. Of course she did this eagerly, arriving at our house as soon as she could get there. Curling up on our bed or on the couch with Heidi lying on top of her, they both slept.

In the ED, the staff took my vital signs, collected some of my blood for testing, and asked me a plethora of questions. I gave them the document I always carry with me in my purse, an abbreviated version of my entire medical history including a list of the prescription medications and supplements I am currently taking, descriptions of on-going conditions I am being treated for, a list of allergies and sensitivities, the dates and outcomes of all my surgeries, the names and contact information of all of my doctors and specialists, the locations and dates of all of my radiographic images, and the dates and locations of all of my emergency department visits with a brief list of diagnostic tests completed at each visit. This may seem redundant, given our access to computer information, but it definitely has helped me time and time again. In this age of shortening appointments, many physicians are not willing to take the time to study a chart like mine that is encyclopedic in length. My five-page document gives them some of the answers they need that I am not able to keep accurately in my head. In the hospital radiology department,we performed a CT scan and shunt X-rays. The ED doctor conversed with my neurosurgeon by phone, and called in an ophthalmologist, as well. The eye doctor performed an ultrasound of my eye. By 11:00 pm we were topping it all off with a MRI, with contrast dye and without. By then we were pretty hungry, tired and ready to be finished with all of this! By the time we left the hospital we knew a lot about what was *not* the problem: hydrocephalus, shunt malfunction, multiple sclerosis, or a brain tumor.

Ken and I went home and crawled into bed. It had been an exhausting and frightening six hours for Ken, and eight hours for me. The question of whether I was going to acquire another diagnosis loomed over me, but I was too tired not to sleep.

Thursday morning arrived too soon. At 8:00 am my cell phone rang, followed by the sound of someone leaving me a voice message. The ophthalmologist's office was following up on the events of the day before. I rolled over in bed and slept another hour. Later, after following my usual morning routine, I picked up the phone and scheduled two appointments, then canceled a routine dental visit I'd scheduled weeks ago. Clean teeth could wait a few more days!

The first appointment of the day was at the neurosurgeon's hospital clinic office to meet with Stephanie, the certified nurse practitioner who had followed my case from my first brain surgery. She was ready with the magnetic device that programs the valve on my brain shunt, changing the pressure setting at which the valve is set to open. She applied a small amount of gel to the area on my head where the valve is located. Then she gently applied the programming apparatus to that area, holding it steadily in place for, maybe, one minute. This painless procedure is completely non-invasive, and only requires removing the gel from my hair when we're finished. The comfortable setting varies from person to person, but is always within a specific range. For some patients, she sets the valve just prior to surgery and never needs to change it again. In more sensitive patients, like me, she may have to tweak the setting in order to provide maximum comfort.

I left the clinic in a good mood, thankful that one more loose end was tied. As I drove up in front of my house, I saw a Cooper's Hawk tearing at his kill, on the ground in our yard. Having striking coloration, Cooper's are handsome and powerful, yet compact, raptors. A family of them has remained in our neighborhood for several years, but this was the first time I'd seen one munching his lunch in my yard. I watched from my car until something scared him off. I wanted to see what his kill was, so I looked intently at the area as I walked past. Only feathers remained of the bird he'd eaten, probably a House Sparrow.

I ate *my* lunch quickly, so I could jump into the car again to drive my reliable, old Saturn to my second appointment. This one would be less comfortable for me. The ophthalmologist wanted to complete a few more tests in his clinic, in order to finalize my diagnosis. Particularly, he wanted to check the field of vision in my affected eye. We had discussed two of the diagnostic possibilities the night before. The first was a serious one: arteritic anterior ischemic optic neuropathy, or AION. This was part of a vascular disease that could effect my whole body and cause blindness. The second possibility and the one he finally chose was non-arteritic anterior ischemic optic neuropathy or NAION. Even he could not say that ten times fast! In essence, my left optic nerve had experienced an ischemic event, or stroke:

the blood flow to it had been briefly cut off for an unknown reason, likely having nothing to do with hydrocephalus, but possibly the result of my sleep apnea. The doctor said I needed to allow it time to heal, but that it may not heal completely, and it may happen again. Another diagnosis to add to my ever-growing list.

I usually went straight home after an encounter such as this one, to research the items from my discussion with my doctor, in order to understand my condition better. This time, however, I canceled my plans for the rest of the day and took a brisk walk with my neighbor friend. A brisk walk is good for relieving stress when paddling a canoe is not available!

My subsequent personal research reminded me that the conditions I was screened for this time in the ED are serious enough to merit all the testing that was done in those six, long hours. I am also reminded of how truly privileged I am compared to so many other people in the world. When I am worried I might be losing my vision, I can make a phone call to a specialist, drive to the specialist's clinic or to an emergency department, request an abundance of tests, receive some of the results immediately, and make an easy appointment for more tests to be done. Someone with more experience than I can relieve my fears and worries the same day or week. Not so in places like Sierra Leone, Africa, or the communities surrounding Lake Titicaca, Bolivia, where a visit to a basic physician could take several days by foot or bicycle to complete, and specialists may be few and far between. Plus, how many people are there who don't have enough money for just their daily needs, let alone medical care, both here in the United States and elsewhere in the world?

I try to never take for granted the gifts I have been given. There is always something to be thankful for.

CHAPTER TWENTY-TWO

Walking On Water: A Faith Journey

THE FOCUS OF this book has been my experience with hydrocephalus and its effects on the rest of my life. My spiritual faith is not separated from the rest of my life in any way. It is an integral part of everything I do, think, say and believe. Every decision made, every joy celebrated involved prayer and communication with God by means of the Holy Spirit, because of the saving sacrifice and love of Jesus Christ. For me, I do not proceed with something unless my spirit, my intellect, my emotions and my will all line up and shout, "YES!" On those occasions when they don't line up, and I choose to go ahead anyway, it is wonderful how God works in and through my mistake to "make all things work together for good" (Romans 8:28).

Truly, God has made my whole life work for good, in spite of my errors in judgment and action. When I look back and realize that I was born with hydrocephalus–or acquired it early in life–yet accomplished all the things I did before my diagnosis in 2006, including earning a college degree, traveling three times to the Andes of Bolivia, South America, on Christian healthcare mission trips, and giving birth to my daughter, I am amazed at what God can and does do in each of us, if we let Him. Many people born with hydrocephalus have significant learning disabilities and struggle to even finish high school, let alone attend college. Yet, I was able to do both without even knowing I had the condition. I struggled, prayed, asked a lot of questions, rejoiced, cried and wondered. Deep in the recesses of my being, I suspected something was different about me. I could tell my thinking process was different from others'. In the 1960's when I was born, hydrocephalus and its effects were not widely discussed among the general public. Now there are support groups, non-profit organizations, educational assistance for those with learning disabilities, and multiple kinds of therapy available to us.

God has been with me every step of my journey, though there were times of major depression and frightening anxiety during which I doubted His presence. I wrote in my journal post-brain surgery: "For awhile now, I've had the sense of seeking something. Seeking answers, seeking truth, seeking a challenge, seeking hope...what was it? Answers. I have so many questions. Why can't I hear Your voice the way I used to? Why am I filled with doubts–yes, even, 'Does God exist?' Throughout my life I have been blessed with unmistakable signs of Your guidance and love. Now You seem silent." In those times, the Holy Spirit would bring to my mind a Bible passage or even just a simple phrase, and I would concentrate on that for days, to keep my mind focused on the positive. Just this year, when I was frustrated with my short-term memory loss, He highlighted, "I will not forget you" from the Old Testament book of Isaiah. What a tremendous gift, to be reminded that in spite of my forgetfulness, He was remembering everything that needed remembering. It gave me peace in the midst of all the fear.

Several Bible passages in the Psalms and books of the Old Testament prophets read, "from birth I have known you" or "I saw you in your mother's womb." How incredibly amazing that there, swimming in my mother's belly, surrounded by her beating heart and nourishing fluids, God knew me. He knew everything about me, down to the cellular level and beyond. Even then He was preparing the way for me. Hundreds of miles away, nine years earlier, someone had invented the first ventriculoperitoneal shunt to treat hydrocephalus. I've now received two versions of that original shunt model.

I firmly believe that God knows every limb, every organ, every tissue, every cell, every atom, every particle or string in our bodies and that make up this world and the universe we live in. He designed and created them all. He wanted to share his love with someone, so He created our world. He made the sun shining, the birds' songs, the plants and animals in all their uniqueness. He says, "I love you," through all those things.

I see God's smile in the smiles of children and hear His laughter in their giggles. I feel Holy Spirit's hugs when a little one runs and jumps into my arms, threatening to knock me over. I feel His encouragement when a mom or a dad tells me their child asked for me to come back to babysit again. I feel Jesus's playful enthusiasm when a dog wags its tail as it sees me on the street, or when a cat rubs against me in greeting.

I enjoyed—and still enjoy--the prayer shawls I was given during recovery. They are warm, like the love of God. They are beautiful, like all that He has created. All of the knots on the tassels remind me of God's many promises to us. The blue-green shawl reminds me of warm Caribbean water and the water of my baptism. The yellow one reminds me of the healing power of light and sun.

God loves me. God loves you. God loves the world God made.

That's enough for me.

HYDROCEPHALUS AND OTHER HELPFUL RESOURCES

There are many resources available, but here is a list to get you started!

The **Hydrocephalus Association** is a wealth of practical and supportive information, educational resources, and grant funding for research. Much information can be downloaded from their website at no charge.

Hydrocephalus Association info@hydroassoc.org 1-888-598-3789

4340 East West Highway, Suite 905 www.hydroassoc.org

Bethesda, MD 20814

An excellent book about hydrocephalus is:

100 Questions & Answers About Hydrocephalus, by Aaron Mohanty, MD

copyright 2012, Jones and Bartlett Learning, LLC

"This book essentially describes various types of hydrocephalus, their symptoms, associated radiologic findings, and available management options for patients with this chronic condition...In simple terms, the purpose of this book can be summarized as *it answers everything that you wanted to ask your doctor but forgot during the appointment.*"

Though I am a member of the **United Methodist Church**, there are many churches and houses of worship that offer spiritual and emotional support in times of crisis and challenge:

www.riverhillsumc.org

River Hills United Methodist Church

11100 River Hills Drive

Burnsville, Minnesota 55337

www.umc.org (The United Methodist Church in America)

For information and resources about **Depression and Anxiety**:

Anxiety and Depression Association of America

https://www.adaa.org/living-with-anxiety/ask-and-learn/resources

For information about the **Minnesota North Country**: www.dnr.state.mn.us

Trees and Shrubs of Minnesota, by Welby R. Smith, Minnesota Department of Natural Resources, University of Minnesota Press, 2008.

Wildflowers of Minnesota Field Guide, by Stan Tekiela, Adventure Publications, Inc., 1999.

Birds in Minnesota, by Robert B. Janssen, University of Minnesota Press, 1992.

Peterson's Field Guide to the Birds of Eastern and Central North America, Houghton Mifflin, 2002.

National Geographic's Field Guide to the Birds of North America, Sixth Edition, by Jon L. Dunn and Jonathan Alderfer, National Geographic, Washington, D. C.

Canoeing the North Country:

Voyageur Canoe Outfitters   1.888.CANOEIT(226.6348)

189 Sag Lake Trail   vco@canoeit.com

Grand Marais, MN 55604

CHRISTIAN BIBLE RESOURCES

From Colossians 1:19 (NRSV)

"For in [Jesus Christ] all the fullness of God was pleased to dwell..."

God came to live with us, in our flesh, willingly and happily, because He loved us so much. He loves each of us body, mind and soul. He wants us to know Who He is.

From Romans 8:35, 37-39 (NRSV)

"Who will separate us from the love of Christ? Will hardship, or distress, or persecution, or famine, or nakedness, or peril, or sword?....No, in all these things we are more than conquerors through him who loved us. For I am convinced that neither death, nor life, nor angels, nor rulers, nor things present, nor things to come, nor powers, nor height, nor depth, nor anything else in all creation, will be able to separate us from the love of God in Christ Jesus our Lord."

From Jeremiah 29:11 (NRSV)

"For surely I know the plans I have for you, says the Lord, plans for your welfare and not for harm, to give you a future with hope."

God always has our welfare in mind. We can hope in Him without reservation.

From <u>Mornings With Jesus 2016</u> (Guideposts and Inspirational Media), p. 266, by Gwen Ford Faulkenberry

"A letter from a reader told me the sad story of a family member's betrayal and the reader's desire to forgive. 'I know Jesus expects more of me,' she wrote. 'I know how toxic resentment can be, so I want to forgive in my heart. But here is my problem. Everyone talks about the importance of forgiveness but no one says how to accomplish it if the other person refuses to participate in repairing things...Can I forgive but not be in the relationship anymore? Is that okay in God's eyes?'

"I believe this is a common problem. We hear all kinds of advice about seventy times seven, turning the other cheek, and so forth, but I think much of our teaching fails to address the difference between forgiveness and reconciliation. What does it mean to forgive 'as in Christ God forgave' us?

"A good illustration of this can be found in the Old Testament story of David and Saul. David loved Saul and wanted a relationship with him. But Saul became jealous of David and tried to kill him numerous times. David forgave Saul and went on loving him. But when it became apparent David could do nothing to mend the relationship, David fled.

"In Jesus, God forgives all of our sin. But because of free will, He does not force us to be reconciled to Him. That's a choice we have to make. It's the same in our relationships with others. We can—and should—forgive the wrongs of others. But reconciliation takes both sides. When one continues in dysfunctional behavior, the other cannot mend the relationship alone. We must get away in order to survive."

From Colossians 3:12-17 (NRSV)

"As God's chosen ones, holy and beloved, clothe yourselves with compassion, kindness, humility, meekness, and patience. Bear with one another and, if anyone has a complaint against another, forgive each other; just as the Lord has forgiven you, so you also must forgive. Above all, clothe yourselves with love, which binds everything together in perfect harmony. And let the peace of Christ rule in your hearts, to which indeed you were called in the one body. And be thankful. Let the word of Christ dwell in you richly; teach and admonish one another in all wisdom; and with gratitude in your hearts sing psalms, hymns, and spiritual songs to God. And whatever you do, in word or deed, do everything in the name of the Lord Jesus, giving thanks to God the Father through him."

From Deuteronomy 20: 1-4 (NRSV)

"When you go out to war against your enemies, and see horses and chariots, an army larger than your own, you shall not be afraid of them; for the Lord your God is with you, who brought you up from the land of Egypt. Before you engage in battle, the priest shall come forward and speak to the troops, and shall say to them: 'Hear, O Israel! Today you are drawing near to do battle against your enemies. Do not lose heart, or be afraid, or panic, or be in dread of them; for it is the Lord your God who goes with you, to fight for you against your enemies, to give you victory.'"

This was a motivational speech for me when I was anxious or afraid. The enemy "horses and chariots" I saw were hydrocephalus, depression, and death. When I pictured them ready to attack me, I would remind myself that God Himself created me and would be with me to fight for me and give me victory over anxiety and fear.

From Psalm 91 (NRSV)

"You who live in the shelter of the Most High,

Who abide in the shadow of the Almighty,

will say to the Lord, 'My refuge and my fortress; my God, in whom I trust.'

For he will deliver you from the snare of the fowler and from the deadly pestilence;

he will cover you with his pinions, and under his wings you will find refuge; his faithfulness is a shield and buckler.

You will not fear the terror of the night, or the arrow that flies by day, or the pestilence that stalks in darkness, or the destruction that wastes at noonday.

"A thousand may fall at your side, ten thousand at your right hand, but it will not come near you.

You will only look with your eyes and see the punishment of the wicked.

"Because you have made the Lord your refuge, the Most High your dwelling place,

no evil shall befall you, no scourge come near your tent.

For he will command his angels concerning you to guard you in all your ways.

On their hands they will bear you up, so that you will not dash your foot against a stone.

You will tread on the lion and the adder, the young lion and the serpent you will trample under foot.

"Those who love me, I will deliver; I will protect those who know my name.

When they call to me, I will answer them; I will be with them in trouble, I will rescue them and honor them.

With long life I will satisfy them, and show them my salvation."

Again, this was a motivational speech, in which the enemies were my medical ills and my anxieties.

From Psalm 139: 1-18 (NRSV)

"O Lord, you have searched me and known me.

You know when I sit down and when I rise up; you discern my thoughts from far away.

You search out my path and my lying down, and are acquainted with all my ways.

Even before a word is on my tongue, O Lord, you know it completely.

You hem me in, behind and before, and lay your hand upon me.

Such knowledge is too wonderful for me; it is so high that I cannot attain it.

"Where can I go from your spirit? Or where can I flee from your presence?

If I ascend to heaven, you are there; if I make my bed in sheol, you are there.

If I take the wings of the morning and settle at the farthest limits of the sea,

even there your hand shall lead me, and your right hand shall hold me fast.

If I say, 'Surely the darkness shall cover me, and the light around me become night,' even the darkness is not dark to you; the night is as bright as the day, for darkness is as light to you.

"For it was you who formed my inward parts; you knit me together in my mother's womb.

I praise you, for I am fearfully and wonderfully made. Wonderful are your works;

that I know very well. My frame was not hidden from you,

when I was being made in secret, intricately woven in the depths of the earth.

Your eyes beheld my unformed substance.

In your book were written all the days that were formed for me, when none of them as yet existed.

How weighty to me are your thoughts, O God! How vast is the sum of them!

I try to count them—they are more than the sand; I come to the end—I am still with you."

One of the most comforting things about God, for me, is that He knows us from beginning to end—and He's not embarrassed!

From Romans 8:26-28 (NRSV)

"Likewise the Spirit helps us in our weakness; for we do not know how to pray as we ought, but that very Spirit intercedes with sighs too deep for words. And God, who searches the heart, knows what is the mind of the Spirit, because the Spirit intercedes for the saints according to the will of God.

We know that all things work together for good for those who love God, who are called according to his purpose."

Sometimes words escape us and prayer seems pointless. In those times, I find it helpful to remember that God, being my creator, understands and knows me better than I know myself. His Holy Spirit prays in our hearts and minds regarding the things we don't have words for. All we need do is acknowledge His presence, and He will take care of the rest.

From Philippians 4:4-9 (NRSV)

"Rejoice in the Lord always; again I will say, Rejoice. Let your gentleness be known to everyone. The Lord is near. Do not worry about anything, but in everything by prayer and supplication with thanksgiving let your requests be made known to God. And the peace of God, which surpasses all understanding, will guard your hearts and your minds in Christ Jesus."

God does not always answer our prayers in the way we expect, but He will ALWAYS answer. Remember to thank Him for His answers, and know that He hears us when we ask Him to explain His answer. He knows that sometimes we just don't understand.

From Philippians 4:11-13, 19 (NRSV)

"Not that I am referring to being in need; for I have learned to be content with whatever I have. I know what it is to have little, and I know what it is to have plenty. In any and all circumstances I have learned the secret of being well-fed and of going hungry, of having plenty and of being in need. I can do all things through him who strengthens me...And my God will fully satisfy every need of yours according to his riches in glory in Christ Jesus. To our God and Father be glory forever and ever. Amen."

This scripture was transcribed inside the cover of the Bible that was given to me when I was confirmed in the Lutheran Church at the age of 14. If only I'd known then what I know now! God's loving care has been with me all the days of my life.

MEDICAL HISTORY TIME LINE

2006   Emergency Department visit for fall on wet concrete and broken nose.

Physician prescribed seizure medication for migraine headaches. This medication also helped sleep apnea a little, so I stopped using SUAD or CPAP devices.

March 5, 2007 Surgical placement of right occipital ventriculoperitoneal (VP) shunt with programmable valve for hydrocephalus.

June 5, 2007   Surgical revision of VP Shunt cranial incision.

July 26, 2008   Last day of employment at the veterinary clinic.

Sept. 26, 2008   (Friday) Began moving my mother-in-law into assisted living facility. Monday was exhausted and slept for several days.

Oct. 3, 2008   (Friday) Visual disturbances. Admitted to the hospital. Surgery to externalize proximal end of brain shunt. Testing of CSF contents.

Oct. 22, 2008   Admitted to the hospital with shunt infection (shunt tap revealed 1+ streptococcus group B).

Oct. 23, 2008   Externalization of proximal end of brain shunt. Reaction to something unknown caused tremors, hives, swelling while hospitalized.

Oct. 26, 2008   Placement of PICC line. Tremors continued, though medication reduced them.

Oct. 28, 2008   Surgical removal of right parietal VP shunt. Replacement with left frontal programmable VP shunt.

November, 2008   Began out-patient speech, cognitive and occupational therapy.

January, 2009   CT scan and immediate hospitalization

February 23, 2009 MRI at neurology clinic.

February 28, 2009 Acute VP Shunt malfunction. Emergency surgical placement of right frontal ventriculostomy secondary to acute VP shunt malfunction.

August, 2009   Completed out-patient speech, cognitive and occupational therapy.

January-March, 2010   Speech and occupational therapy at a specialty Parkinson's center.

March, 2010   Severe back pain. Two herniated lumbar discs found. Steroid injection and physical therapy.

October 5, 2010   Routine maintenance CT scan of Left VP brain shunt

December 22, 2010   Fell on ice/ ED visit. Fractured right proximal fibula and sprained right ankle.

May 9, 2012   Routine maintenance CT scan and shunt x-ray series. Adjustment of valve setting.

July 12–Sep. 19, 2012   Physical Therapy for epicondylitis and DeQuervains tenosynitis (elbow and wrist).

September 21, 2012   Emergency Dept. visit for sprained ankle.

December 28, 2012 Discontinuation of anti-tremor medication and CT scan of brain.

July 24, 2014   Pituitary blood tests confirm post-menopausal status.

August 1, 2014 Emergency Dept. visit for right upper quadrant abdominal pain. Abdominal ultrasound normal, but liver function blood tests elevated.

August 28-September 25, 2014 Liver   and   abdominal   tests   at gastroenterology specialists.

PRESENTATION FOR HYDROCEPHALUS WALK

Twin Cities, Minnesota

September 23, 2012

LESLI:

Hi, I'm Lesli Anderson. Today I'm walking with the group "WeAreThree".

Last year on a chilly Fall morning at the Hydrocephalus Association WALK, three women met each other for the first time. Chris was walking because she was diagnosed early in life with hydrocephalus and has had many, many surgeries to place ventriculoperitoneal shunts throughout her lifetime. Mary was walking because she went through years of searching and false diagnoses before the doctors figured out that she has a Chiari Malformation with hydrocephalus. I am the third woman who was, unknown to anyone at the time, born with a constriction of the Aqueduct of Sylvius, a portion of the brain connected to the ventricles. But this was not discovered until five years ago. Last year, I was walking because I had just turned 50 and recovered from receiving my second VP shunt after being in and out of the hospital with complications after the first shunt.

Discovering each other was amazing, because each of us acquired hydrocephalus in a different way, and each of us is an adult in a different stage of life. A young single woman starting her teaching career, a middle-aged woman changing careers and raising a family, and a middle-aged career woman with grown children. We spent hours together talking about our medical experiences. It is so reassuring to have someone to talk with about hydrocephalus, who has no trouble pronouncing the word or spelling it, who doesn't need to ask, "What's syphalic....whatever you said?" We discovered that though we were different, many of our feelings and thoughts about our medical experiences were pretty similar. We immediately decided we would try to share this support and encouragement with others.

And we did! We advertised meetings and talked with people one-on-one who had been diagnosed with hydrocephalus. We even had a spaghetti dinner and game night for our families and friends. It's frightening to be told there is something out-of-sorts with your brain. We learned that many elderly people have hydrocephalus that has been prematurely diagnosed as Alzheimer's or Parkinson's Disease. We've learned to be comfortable with CT Scans, MRI's, and bumpy shaved heads!

Brief Talk for River Hills United Methodist Church 50th Anniversary

- Hi! My name is Lesli Anderson, and I am a member here at River Hills Church. For the past 5 years I have had a calling about which I'd like to share with you.

- Let's start with a short biology lesson. Minnesota is known as the Land of 10,000 Lakes and is the birthplace of the mighty Mississippi River. I live in Minneapolis, the City of Lakes, near 4 lakes that are connected by Minnehaha Creek. Minnehaha means "curling waters" in the Dahcota language, though it is frequently mistranslated as "laughing waters". Minnehaha Creek eventually empties into the Mississippi River at Minnehaha Falls. The Mississippi is the backbone of our country.

- Inside your brain there are 4 compartments called ventricles. Think of these as the 4 lakes I just mentioned. Filled with cerebrospinal fluid, they are connected by several narrow passageways. Cerebrospinal fluid, or CSF, flows between the lateral ventricles, to the third ventricle, through the Aqueduct of Sylvius, and into the fourth ventricle, then into the narrow space surrounding the brain and the spinal cord. This is similar to how Minnehaha Creek flows from lake to lake into the Mississippi River.

- The CSF that bathes our brains provides important nutrients, helps clean out cellular waste, and protects our brains by cushioning them. Without it, we would experience major brain trauma every time we bumped our heads. Of course, it also helps to have a bony skull as armor.

- Some time late in 1960, I was conceived and grew inside my mother's womb. Psalm 139 says I was being fearfully and wonderfully made. No one knows exactly when or how it happened, but at some point something went wrong. I was born in September of 1961 with a hidden defect in my brain. Even the doctors at the time didn't know it was there, so as I grew and my body developed, my brain compensated for the defect in order to function. (Now, **that is** being fearfully and wonderfully made!)

- Fast forward to 2006. I had been married 20 years to Ken and we had a 13-year-old daughter, Kaitlyn. I had a Bachelor of Science degree in biology with a minor in chemistry. I had worked in medical laboratories and was then working as an assistant at a Veterinary hospital in Minneapolis, while attending college in the evenings in order to earn the title of Veterinary Technician. I was beginning to feel that I had finally found my calling in life. Providing medical care to animals seemed to use all of my previous life experiences and my faith in God, as well.

- Each evening at the Vet hospital, we swept and mopped the concrete floor of the entire hospital, preparing to go home for the night. One evening, while closing, and in spite of trying to be very careful, I slipped on the wet floor and fell full force on my face. I came away from a hospital emergency department with only a broken nose, however, inside my brain something had changed as a result of that fall, but, again, no one knew about it. My laughing waters were no longer laughing. I began to have more and more headaches, severe ones sometimes lasting several days at a time. My family doctor and I treated the pain with various medications for migraines.

- Finally, in desperation I requested that a CAT scan be done. I waited nervously for the doctor to call with the result. It led to an MRI and a visit to a neurosurgeon. The neurosurgeon reported that it was clear on the MRI that I had congenital hydrocephalus, decompensated by my fall. This was how I learned at the age of 45 that I was born with hydrocephalus.

- Hydrocephalus is an abnormal accumulation of cerebrospinal fluid within those ventricles in the brain I mentioned earlier–remember the lakes? It is diagnosed by several key symptoms, and can occur in anyone at any age. It can be misdiagnosed as Parkinson's Disease or Alzheimer's.

- It is a chronic medical condition with no cure, effecting a million people per year. Approximately 6,000 new babies are born with hydrocephalus every year in the U. S. The treatment leaves many people with compromised quality of life and a lifetime of brain surgeries and worry. The most common treatment is surgical implantation of a device called a shunt. A shunt is a flexible tube and valve system that diverts the flow of CSF away from the head into another part of the body where it can be absorbed. Shunts have not changed significantly since the 1950's and a high failure and revision rate is common.

- I have now had six surgical procedures performed for the purpose of giving me relief from hydrocephalus, all within about a two-year period. My first shunt failed and became infected after a year and a half, possibly causing some brain damage. To give you some perspective, there are three days during this period of time that I do not remember. Everything I know about them was told to me by my family. The next shunt, which replaced the first, malfunctioned within 4 months of placement. The surgeon was able to repair the shunt, and I still have it today. Many people with hydrocephalus have had more than a dozen brain surgeries; more than 100 is not unheard of. Shunt failure is so common that it is practically expected within the first 6 months, in spite of dedicated efforts to eliminate malfunction and infection. There are no medications or non-surgical procedures available to treat hydrocephalus.

- And so, in 2010 I began volunteering for the Hydrocephalus Association. The volunteers and staff provide education, support, and research funding to patients and physicians all over the world. Please come to my table in the Fellowship Hall to learn more about the Hydrocephalus Association.

- Besides learning more about the amazing and wonderful body with which God has truly blessed me, He has shown me how "all things work together for good, with those who love Him, who are called according to His purpose" and I am learning with the Apostle Paul how to be content in all circumstances and that I **can** do all things through Christ who strengthens me. One interesting thing I have noticed is that if you spend a lifetime immersed in Scripture and make it part of your very fiber, even when you are unconscious or under anesthesia, God's words are there with you.

- My brain and my body are God's gift to me. He also gave me a sense of humor, for which I am most grateful. And I have learned that I am surrounded by a deeply loving church family and biological family, who have stuck with me through all the medications and surgeries. They are Jesus's hands and feet in the world.

Brief Presentation

THE LAKES IN MY HEAD

Minnesota is known as the Land of 10,000 Lakes and is the birthplace of the mighty Mississippi River. I live in Minneapolis, the City of Lakes, near Lake Minnetonka, Lake Pamela, Lake Nokomis, Lake Hiawatha and the creek that connects all of them, Minnehaha Creek. Minnehaha means "curling waters" in the Dahcota language, though it is frequently mistranslated as "laughing waters" (but that's a whole other story). Minnehaha Creek eventually empties into the Mississippi River at Minnehaha Falls. The Mississippi is the backbone of our country.

Inside your head there are four compartments called ventricles. Think of these as the four lakes I just mentioned. Filled with cerebrospinal fluid, they are connected by several narrow passageways. Cerebrospinal fluid, or CSF, flows between the lateral ventricles, to the third ventricle, through the Aqueduct of Sylvius, and into the fourth ventricle, then into the narrow space surrounding the brain and the spinal cord. This is similar to how Minnehaha Creek flows from lake to lake into the Mississippi River.

I hope you see now why I call this "The Lakes in My Head". Each of you has lakes in your head, too. The CSF that bathes our brains provides important nutrients, helps clean out cellular waste, and protects our brains by cushioning them. Without it, we would experience major brain trauma every time we bumped our heads. Of course, it also helps to have a bony skull as armor.

Some time late in 1960, I was conceived and grew inside my mother's womb. Psalm 139 says I was being fearfully and wonderfully made. No one knows exactly when or how it happened, but at some point something went wrong. I was born in September of 1961 with a hidden defect in my brain. Even the doctors at the time didn't know it was there, so as I grew and my body developed, my brain compensated for the defect in order to function. I think that's pretty amazing. That's being wonderfully made.

I looked and behaved just like any other little girl growing up in the 60's, except I had trouble with frequent, severe headaches. They seemed to be connected to the changes in weather so common to living in Minnesota. On a hot, humid summer day, while outside playing, I would develop a severe headache and come in the house crying. As I grew older, I learned ways to avoid the headaches, but I also had to avoid some of the fun activities I enjoyed doing with my friends.

Fast forward to 2006. By the age of 45 years, I had been married 20 years to Ken and we had a 13-year-old daughter, Kaitlyn, who was attending middle school in Minneapolis. I had a Bachelor of Science degree in biology with a minor in chemistry and a strong interest in biochemistry. I had worked in medical laboratories and was then working as a veterinary assistant at a pet hospital in Minneapolis. I was attending college in the evenings in order to earn the title of Veterinary Technician. I was beginning to feel that I had finally found my calling in life. Providing medical care to animals seemed to use all of my previous life experiences and my faith in God, as well.

Each evening at the Pet Hospital, we swept and mopped the concrete floor of the entire hospital, preparing to go home for the night. One evening, while closing, and in spite of trying to be very careful, I slipped on the wet floor and fell full force on my face. It happened so quickly and unexpectedly, that as I lay on the floor with my face down I began to laugh. The rest of the hospital staff gathered around me with concern, surely wondering why I was laughing and not crying! One of the veterinarians offered to take me to an emergency department, and I agreed to go, but called my husband to ask him to drive me there.

The hospital emergency staff acted quickly as soon as they found out that I could possibly have a concussion from a fall. After taking x-rays of my head, it was determined that I did not seem to have a concussion, but I had definitely broken my nose. All manner of care was applied to my sore nose and instructions given for further care at home.

Inside my brain, however, something had changed as a result of that fall, but no one knew it at the time. My laughing waters were no longer laughing.

I began to have more and more headaches, severe ones sometimes lasting several days at a time. My family doctor and I treated the pain with various medications for migraines. Finally, in desperation I requested that a CAT scan be done of my sinuses, thinking this was some bizarre form of sinus infection. The CT scan done, I waited for the doctor to call with the result.

The call I received was not the one I was expecting. "Yes, you have a really nasty sinus infection, Lesli..." was what I was expecting to hear from my doctor. Instead, I heard, "There is no infection, Lesli. However, the radiologist did notice something unusual on the scan. He is recommending you have an MRI to get us a better look." After the MRI, the usual wait for results made me nervous. Days of wondering what could be so important that the radiologist would recommend an MRI for it followed. One evening, after being unable to reach me at home, my doctor called me at the animal hospital, ironically, just as we were cleaning up for the night. "You have hydrocephalus, Lesli, and the only treatment I know of is surgical placement of a shunt. I will refer you to a neurosurgeon so you can discuss it with him; he will know much more about it than I do." The neurosurgeon said it was clear on the MRI that my condition was congenital, but that my fall traumatized my brain so that it couldn't compensate for the hydrocephalus any more. This was how I learned I was born with hydrocephalus, but no one ever knew it!

Hydrocephalus? I had imagined a malignant tumor, or a really nasty infection, but never hydrocephalus. I thought babies were born with it, not knowing that adults could have it, too. Hydrocephalus is an abnormal accumulation of cerebrospinal fluid within those ventricles I mentioned earlier, inside the brain. It creates several key symptoms, and can occur in anyone at any age. It can be misdiagnosed as Parkinson's Disease or Alzheimer's.

Hydrocephalus, a chronic medical condition with no cure and a 50-year-old treatment, effects a million people per year. Approximately six thousand new babies are born with hydrocephalus every year in the United States. The treatment leaves many people with compromised quality of life and a lifetime of brain surgeries and worry. The most common treatment is surgical implantation of a device called a shunt. A shunt is a flexible tube and valve system that diverts the flow of CSF away from the head into another part of the body where it can be absorbed. Shunts have not changed significantly since the 1950's and a high failure and revision rate is common. Many people with hydrocephalus have had more than a dozen brain surgeries; more than 100 brain surgeries is not unheard of.

I have now had six separate surgical procedures performed for the purpose of giving me relief from decompensated hydrocephalus, all within about a two-year period. My first shunt failed and became infected after a year and a half, possibly causing some brain damage. To give you some perspective, there are three days during this period of time that I do not remember. Everything I know about them was told to me by my family. The next shunt, which replaced the first, malfunctioned within four months of placement. The surgeon was able to repair the shunt, and I still have that shunt today. My experiences with shunts is not unique. The brain shunt is one of only three surgical procedures available to treat hydrocephalus; there are no medications or non-surgical procedures available to treat it. Shunt failure is so common that it is practically expected within the first six months, in spite of dedicated efforts to eliminate malfunction and infection.

The cost of shunt surgeries to treat hydrocephalus in the U.S. exceeds $1 billion per year, not including any rehabilitative therapy or educational accommodation. Accurately diagnosing and treating the 375,000 adults over 60 years old suspected to have normal pressure hydrocephalus could save Medicare $184 million over five years.

I began volunteering for the Hydrocephalus Association in 2010. The Hydrocephalus Association was founded in 1983 and incorporated as a nonprofit in 1986. It is governed by a Board of Directors, and employs about eight staff members. It receives no government funding. Over 70% of its funding comes from individual donations and memberships. The volunteers and staff of HA are very busy each year providing education, support, and research funding to patients and physicians involved with hydrocephalus.

The Hydrocephalus Association is the largest non-profit, non-governmental fund-er of hydrocephalus research in the U.S.

Besides learning more about the amazing and wonderful body that God has truly blessed me with, He has shown me how "all things work together for good, with those who love Him, who are called according to His purpose" and I am learning with the Apostle Paul how to be content in all circumstances and that "I can do all things through Christ who strengthens me." One interesting thing I have noticed is that if you spend a lifetime immersed in Scripture and make it part of your very fiber, even when you are unconscious or under anesthesia, the words are there with you. When you spend lots of time with Jesus, even your dreams bring you closer to Him.

I love my brain and my body. They are God's gift to me. He also gave me a sense of humor, for which I am most grateful. And I have learned that I am surrounded by a deeply loving church family and biological family, who have stuck with me through all the medications and surgeries. They are Jesus's hands and feet in the world.

BIBLIOGRAPHY

Here If You Need Me, A True Story, by Kate Braestrup, Back Bay Books; Little, Brown and Company, 2007.

Excerpts taken from In the Likeness Of God by Dr. Paul Brand and Philip Yancey Copyright © 2004 by Philip Yancey. Used by permission of Zondervan. www.zondervan.com.

Holy Bible: New Revised Standard Version Reference Bible, Zondervan Corporation, 1990.

All scripture quotations except where noted are from this version. Copyright 1989 by the National Council of the Churches of Christ in the United States of America. Used by permission. All rights reserved world wide.

Life Application Study Bible New International Version, Tyndale House Publishers and Zondervan Publishing House, 1991.

The "NIV" and "New International Version" are trademarks registered in the United States Patent and Trademark Office by Biblica, Inc.

Taber's Cyclopedic Medical Dictionary, F. A. Davis Company, Twentieth Edition, 2005.

Webster's New World College Dictionary, IDG Books Worldwide, Inc., Fourth Edition, 2000.

Trees and Shrubs of Minnesota, by Welby R. Smith, Minnesota Department of Natural Resources, University of Minnesota Press, 2008.

Wildflowers of Minnesota Field Guide, by Stan Tekiela, Adventure Publications, Inc., 1999.

Peterson's Field Guide to the Birds of Eastern and Central North America, Houghton Mifflin, 2002.

National Geographic's Field Guide to the Birds of North America, Sixth Edition, by Jon L. Dunn and Jonathan Alderfer, National Geographic, Washington, D. C.

National Center For Learning Disabilities websites

www.ncld.org

understood.org

Printed in the United States
By Bookmasters